Steps to Heaven

STAR NOBLE

Dreamspinner Press

Published by
DREAMSPINNER PRESS

5032 Capital Circle SW, Suite 2, PMB# 279, Tallahassee, FL 32305-7886 USA
http://www.dreamspinnerpress.com/

Steps to Heaven
© 2015 Star Noble.

Cover Art
© 2015 Paul Richmond.
http://www.paulrichmondstudio.com
Cover content is for illustrative purposes only and any person depicted on the cover is a model.

ISBN: 978-1-63216-375-2
Digital ISBN: 978-1-63216-376-9
Library of Congress Control Number: 2014951375
First Edition January 2015

Printed in the United States of America
∞
This paper meets the requirements of
ANSI/NISO Z39.48-1992 (Permanence of Paper).

My special thanks go to my Senior Editor, Sue Adams,
for her patience and support.
I also want to thank my other editors, Nicole and Barbara.
They all did a great job.

Chapter One

STEVE RANDALL, a detective in the Culver City Police Department, leaned back in the passenger seat and let out a contented sigh. "We did a good job, didn't we?" He punched Bob Curry playfully in the side.

"Hey, I'm driving here!" his best friend and partner Bob complained with a smile. "I admit, you were great lunging out of that closet and overpowering Linda's stalker." He cast Steve a proud glance.

"Yeah, we caught the lunatic before he could seriously injure Linda. Your former classmate is a gorgeous woman." Steve looked at Bob expectantly. Was Bob in love with her? Steve had noticed Bob holding Linda protectively while she cried in his arms, fearing that the stalker would hurt her.

"In college, everybody wanted to be Linda Thornton's friend." Bob looked at him, his blue eyes sparkling. "She's still lovable, and I'm glad she's safe now." He turned into a side street and slowed down, looking left and right.

"What are you looking for?" Steve asked, confused. "I thought we were going to my house to relax and celebrate a closed case? I have beer and—"

"I'm looking for a photo studio. 'Fashion Photos, where promising careers start.'" Bob checked both sides of the street, lined with warehouses and closed shops.

"Hey, I'm a great model," Steve joked, waggling his butt and moving his arms like a dancer.

"Dummy," Bob scolded. "Linda asked me to see her at a photo shoot she's doing tonight before she returns to Philadelphia. She's become a well-known model." Bob stopped his car.

"Okay, I understand." Steve got serious. "And how do I get home? Take a taxi?"

"What're you talking about? You're coming with me, of course. Linda wants to thank you for your courageous intervention in catching the stalker." Bob got out of the comfortable old Mercedes.

Steve followed, happy that he could be with his friend. When had he gotten so dependent on him? They'd worked as a team now for five years, and the shared experiences had brought them closer together.

"It must be over there." Bob crossed the street and walked toward an entrance. A silver sign next to the door read "Fashion Photos."

They stepped into the photo studio and heard laughter and voices coming from a room to the left. Bob opened the door and peered inside.

A man in tight black pants and a white silk shirt moved around a female model. It was Linda Thornton. He held a camera, trying to find the right angle. A jazzy beat was filling the room, and the photographer swayed to the music with a smile, the bright arc lamps reflecting off his bald head.

Bob and Steve entered the room hesitantly, waving at Linda.

She waved back. "Guys, you can wait over there at my dressing table. This is Randolph Foreman, the best photographer in the world!"

Randolph focused on his model. Linda was wearing a thin blouse and a wide skirt. A wind machine was blowing the fabric up, revealing her long legs.

He took photo after photo. "Good. Now we need some polarity, something for you to work against." Randolph looked around, noticing the two visitors for the first time.

Leaning against Linda's dressing table, Bob and Steve watched the photo shoot.

"We need you!" Randolph exclaimed.

"You what?" Bob asked.

Steve stood openmouthed, not understanding what Randolph wanted.

"Go, stand by her. Don't be shy. You can do it." Randolph ran over and pulled the resisting Bob away from the dressing table.

"Trust me. Trust me." Randolph also grabbed Steve's arm and dragged him toward the stage too, where Linda stood smiling.

"Stand by the beauty. Yes, yes." Randolph was obviously fascinated by his idea.

"I can't. I'm shy," Bob objected when the photographer placed him next to Linda.

"Yeah, yeah, I know you're shy," said Randolph, not at all impressed. He stood back to envision the shot for a moment.

"And you, over there." He motioned Steve to the other side.

Linda slung her arm around Steve's shoulder, the fan at their feet blowing her blonde hair back. She smiled, looking relaxed and happy.

"And you do angry. *Angry*." Randolph stepped back and brought his camera into position.

Deciding to make the best of it, Steve put a grim expression on his face. He met Bob's eyes, and after a moment of hesitation, Bob matched his look. Steve nodded, content. They were feeling good with Linda snuggling in close to them.

"You're a vision of delight, honey," Randolph crooned at Linda. He took a series of shots, smiling all the while. "You did quite good, guys. Cut, over!" Randolph straightened, regarding the group with appreciation.

"Finally!" Bob breathed a sigh of relief and fled from the stage. He caught his foot on a cable and went down with a thud.

"Bob, watch your step!" Linda said, startled.

"Boy, you can't get away fast enough, can you?" Steve bent down to help Bob up. "You're so clumsy, buddy," he whispered in Bob's ear.

"Too cute!" Randolph said from behind. He looked at the two men with admiration.

Bob blushed and hissed, "Let's get out of here!" He dragged Steve with him.

"Why the hurry, boys?" Linda asked. She turned to Randolph. "Thanks for the shoot. You're the best." She dropped a kiss on his cheek.

"Love you, honey," he crooned, but his eyes were on the departing detectives. They were almost at the door when Randolph caught up. "Don't leave, please," he begged. "Don't know your name, but I've just found my latest model." He beamed at Steve, examining him from head to toe.

Now it was Steve's turn to blush. "We're cops, not models." He pulled Bob out of the room, but Randolph didn't give up that easily.

"Guys, have mercy! Enrico, the star of my latest photo series, left me without any reason. I'm heartbroken and in need of a substitute. You"—he looked at Steve with sparkling eyes—"have the perfect body for the next swimwear summer collection."

"No way, Mr....?"

Steve went out the door. Linda went after him.

"Listen, Steve. Randolph is an old friend of mine," she said, standing in front of him so he couldn't get by. "You've been so kind to help me. Now, would you do this guy a favor? I'm sure he'll pay you really well." She looked at her former classmate Bob, searching for backup.

Bob shrugged, looking more relaxed now that the attention was off him.

Three pairs of eyes watched Steve Randall.

Randolph said, "Please, do me the favor. Um, what's your name—Steve? Be my model for this photo shoot. It won't last long. It's for my company's next collection. If I don't get a model right now, my ass is on the line." He looked down, sighing deeply. He was a pitiful sight.

"Hey, buddy, it can't be too hard," Bob said. "Linda and I are going to have a drink, and we'll pick you up afterward." He smiled at Linda, and both of them looked expectantly at Steve.

"You think I'm that easy? That I'd make a fool of myself posing half-naked? Forget it." Steve scowled.

Linda put her hand on his shoulder. "Steve, I can easily picture you in a Speedo. You're slender, with muscles in all the right places." She glanced down at his body, undressing him with her eyes.

"Linda's right. You have the perfect body for the next swimwear collection, Steve," Bob said with an encouraging smile.

"You want me to expose myself to the camera? What kind of a friend are you?" Steve sounded panicky.

"Guys, listen." Randolph came closer, looking around as if worried they would be overheard. "I shouldn't talk about it here," he said with a confidential hush in his voice. "But if you let me off the hook and help me with the photo shoot, I could be useful and give you some information about the drug activities in town lately."

"Randy?" A young man peeked through the adjacent door, his dark eyes wandering from Steve to Bob and back to Randolph. "Sorry to interrupt, but we have to meet Sanders at eight thirty. Are you finished here?"

Randolph looked at Steve with pleading eyes. "Would you help me? It wouldn't take long."

Steve exchanged glances with Bob, and he saw the approval in his friend's eyes. *Do it, buddy, I think we can take advantage of Randolph as a new snitch. I'll be back soon. Okay?*

"It's a deal," Steve said reluctantly, looking at his watch. "Don't have a lot of time, though. Let's start right away."

"You saved my ass!" Randolph shouted and turned to the young man waiting impatiently at the door. "Chris, you know Enrico's not coming around anymore." He pointed to Steve. "I have to do the photo shoot with a new model. Tell Sanders I'll join both of you later tonight. I'm busy right now. *Ciao.*" He blew Chris a good-bye kiss and turned to Steve. "Your dark hair looks gorgeous. I mean we could use some pomade to make it look wet. And...."

"Bye, and good luck." Linda kissed Steve on the cheek and whispered, "Thanks. Randolph is such a sweetheart, and I know you'll do just great."

"I hope you don't quit your job on the force for a career as a top model," Bob smirked and sidestepped when Steve pretended to kick his butt.

Steve was relieved when Bob and Linda left the room. He wanted to get the photo session over with as soon as possible.

"Where do I start, Randolph?" he asked, checking the studio more thoroughly. There were a lot of cameras and spotlights in the room. In one corner, he could see a blue sheet hanging from the ceiling to the floor.

"Over there." Randolph pointed to the corner with the blue sheet. "I can't thank you enough. The longer I look at you, the more I'm convinced you are a better model than Enrico. Your body—"

"Let's concentrate on business." Steve felt awkward and uncomfortable under Randolph's scrutinizing gaze.

"That's exactly what I plan to do." Randolph licked his lips. He motioned Steve over to a door that led to a little room. "Get undressed, and I'll be right back with the collection. Make yourself at home."

Randolph patted him lightly on the shoulder and disappeared, closing the dressing room door behind him.

Steve sat down on the chair and looked in the mirror. He couldn't believe what he was about to do. Letting someone take pictures of him, clad only in swimming trunks. It was all Bob's fault. When Linda had convinced Steve to do the photo session, Bob had probably only agreed to impress her.

Now, while Bob was having a drink with a beautiful woman, Steve had to wait in a shabby room with nothing but a mirror and a little table covered in tubes and pots, a chair, and a bench full of clothes. What if he left, unnoticed, through the back door?

"Hey, aren't you ready yet?" Randolph entered the room, his arms full of swimwear. He shoved Linda's discarded dresses off the bench and deposited the bathing suit collection on top. "Get undressed, so I can put some makeup on your skin. It looks better in the spotlights. But I must admit, you have such a great, dark tan, we'll only have to apply a little bit."

"Are you kidding?" Steve got up and tried to get past Randolph to the door.

"No worries, Officer." Randolph smiled. You'll see, you'll look terrific!"

Before Steve could react, Randolph had reached for Steve's belt and started to unbuckle it.

"Hey, what are you doing?" Steve pushed Randolph's hands away. "I can do it by myself, capeesh?"

"Okay. See you right away. We'll start with the Bermudas. Call me when you're ready. In the meantime, I'll do some preparations." Randolph stood waiting.

Steve got the impression Randolph was waiting for him to get rid of his clothes. Not moving, his hands still on his belt, Steve gazed back at the photographer until he left the room, looking disappointed.

Watching the door, Steve hurried to get out of his jeans. He cursed himself for having worn his briefs with tiger print that morning. He felt embarrassed. Hastily he changed into the bright blue Bermudas Randolph had put on top of the pile. They didn't look that bad on him, Steve had to admit as he checked himself in the mirror.

The door opened. "You want to go swimming with your shirt on, Detective? Come on, let me help you out of this, and then you can sit down." Randolph came behind him and lifted up the shirt. Seconds later Steve stood bare-chested.

"Trust my hands." Randolph smiled and pushed Steve gently into the makeup chair.

"What?"

Steve wanted to ask more, but the photographer silenced him. Randolph poured a liquid from a small pot onto his hands and applied it to Steve's shoulders.

"Hey, what are you doing? What kind of makeup is that?" Steve looked in the mirror. A shiny fluid covered his shoulders.

"Body oil." Randolph trailed his hands over Steve's upper body, using less oil on the furry chest. "You look beautiful, Sergeant. Now your legs. Turn around so I can take care of them."

"My legs too?" Steve felt more awkward when Randolph moved his hands up Steve's calves, rubbing the oil onto the skin. He was glad he was wearing Bermudas as it wouldn't be necessary to put the oil on his thighs.

"Later we'll work on your thighs," Randolph muttered, finishing by drying his hands on a towel.

"Can we start now?" Steve couldn't wait to get out of the small room. Randolph made him feel crowded. It occurred to him that with Bob he had never felt so uncomfortable. They had been in situations when they had to hide in a small space together—recently, for example, as they waited in Linda's closet for her stalker to appear.

He had been so close to Bob, their limbs entangled and breaths mingling, and he had felt safe and protected. Being with Bob had never given him any reason to feel awkward. They had even slept in the same bed that time Bob's apartment had to be fumigated because of termites. Steve remembered the good feeling of being close to his partner and best friend. He smiled.

"A penny for your thoughts, Lieutenant." Randolph's words drew Steve back to the present.

"Detective Randall," Steve corrected.

"Close your eyes, Detective, so I can work on your face. That's fine." Randolph applied some makeup and powder on Steve's face.

"Let me call you Steve, please." Randolph patted Steve's cheek lightly. He stashed the cosmetic away in a large box, grabbed another pot, and filled his palms with whatever it contained.

"No more oil," Steve protested.

"No oil. Only a bit of gel to make your beautiful hair look wet," Randolph said. He drew his hands through Steve's hair. "Just perfect. We're done. Now, let's get started. You see the blue curtain in the studio? Go there and pose in front. Pretend you are on the beach enjoying yourself. I'll tell you what to do. You just look happy and relaxed."

"That's easier said than done," Steve mumbled, adjusting the waistband of his Bermudas.

Randolph directed his camera on his new model and checked the light meter before fiddling with the f-stop and focal length.

Steve stepped in front of the blue curtain, feeling insecure and exposed. He tried to distract himself by thinking about Bob and Linda relaxing in a café, chatting and having a good time while he was stuck doing the damned photo shoot.

"You'll do great, Steve," Randolph encouraged. "Here's a ball. Pretend to throw it, but don't hit me." Randolph giggled and tossed him a red, yellow, and blue beach ball.

Steve played with the ball, bouncing it gingerly. He could almost picture himself on the beach, enjoying a ball game. He and Bob often went down to the sand to….

"That smile turns me on. Fabulous!" Randolph took several quick shots, the camera flash blinding Steve's eyes. He beamed at Steve. "That was promising! There are two more pairs of Bermuda shorts before we change to the trunks."

"Really? I did good?" Steve couldn't believe it. *Wait until Bob hears about that!*

He walked back into the dressing room, feeling Randolph's gaze follow him. At least the photographer didn't follow him inside, and he could change without being disturbed.

Step by step Steve was beginning to feel more relaxed. After all, he was doing this to gain information from a new snitch. For the last couple of months, the Culver City police department had dealt with more drug overdose deaths than usual. Rumor had it there was a new drug on the streets called Blue Rocket. The new drug made the user feel high and powerful in an instant. But no one knew who was behind the organization producing it. Obviously, this new drug was dangerous, and Steve planned to have a word with the photographer when the shoot was over.

He was just about to put on the swimming trunks when Randolph abruptly entered the dressing room. Seeing Steve's exposed ass, he gave an appreciative whistle.

His cheeks burning, Steve hid his embarrassment and pulled the trunks on.

Randolph smiled apologetically. "Some more oil for your thighs, m'dear." He squirted a dollop out of the bottle and filled his palms with the oil. Before Steve could protest, Randolph touched the skin above Steve's knees.

"Let me do it, okay?" Steve opened his hands, and Randolph let the oil drip into Steve's palm.

A grin lit Randolph's face. "Detective, er, Steve, admit it. I turn you on, don't I? You're afraid my touch will give you feelings you don't want to show right now…." He rubbed the rest of the oil off his hand. "Don't worry. I don't plan to go to that boring meeting with Chris and my boss. We have all the time in the world to get to know each other better. Come on, let's finish the shoot as quickly as possible."

Oil dripping from his hands, Steve stared openmouthed at Randolph's back as he disappeared out of the dressing room. Turned on? Who? Was this guy gay?

It took all Steve's acting abilities to look happy and relaxed while being photographed, knowing that Randolph obviously had a crush on him. Steve felt more exposed—the swim trunks seemed so revealing.

"Show it to me!" Randolph said cheerfully, snapping a picture as Steve pretended to run on the beach. "Yeah, be proud of yourself! You feel good. Turn to the side, yes, that's it!"

Steve complied, feeling like nothing more than a sex object.

"And now spread your legs as if you intend to jump on something."

Randolph's excitement made Steve cringe. If Bob knew.... *Buddy, I miss you, your presence, your protectiveness. What about picking me up? Didn't you say you and Linda would only go to the café for a short while? You should be back by now.*

"Cut! We're done." Randolph beamed at his model. "Get the oil off your body. The showers are at the end of the hall."

Steve yanked a discarded jacket off a bench to cover himself. Damn, this had been a terrible idea. He wanted to escape, and fast. Randolph's smile turned seductive, but Steve shook his head.

"I told you, I'm in a hurry," he said tightly. "My friend should be here any minute to pick me up." Steve ignored the disappointment in Randolph's eyes and hurried to the dressing room. He closed the door behind him and grabbed a towel to wipe the oil off his body. As he got out of the trunks, he almost stumbled and cursed.

"You need any help?"

He could hear Randolph hovering outside the door. Steve suppressed another hiss and grabbed his briefs and jeans to get dressed. He was about to button his shirt when Randolph knocked on the door and peeked in.

"Hey, gorgeous. Let's have a drink together, at least, and relax now that we've done the work. I promised you some information." Randolph motioned Steve to follow him down the hall.

Reluctant to be alone with him, Steve still needed the info on the drug. He buttoned his shirt to the neck and walked down the hall behind Randolph.

Steve checked his watch. It was after six o'clock. Bob should have picked him up by now. On the other hand, they needed Randolph as a snitch. With any luck, he could help them with some useful insider information about Blue Rocket. Steve would just have to grin and bear the photographer's advances. He quickened his pace.

Opposite the showers, a little door led to a small office. Randolph unlocked it. "Come in. We won't be disturbed. Chris and the rest of the staff are gone by now." He flopped into a chair with a finger to his lips. "What I'm going to tell you is strictly confidential. If anyone knew about our little conversation, I could be in big trouble." He glanced around as if expecting Chris to return at any moment.

"Don't worry," Steve reassured him. He lounged against the doorframe, as far from Randolph as possible.

"We've lost some of our models during the last few months." The photographer shook his head with a frown. "They just didn't come back, and I have no idea why." He leaned closer, whispering. "I know for sure that they are members of Steps to Heaven. It's a new club, and rumors say there is a new drug available for members. They say Blue Rocket is a wonder drug that makes you feel on top of the world." Randolph stood, looked deeply into Steve's eyes, and inched even closer, which wasn't difficult in the tiny office. "And," he continued, still whispering, "you get an insatiable urge for sex." His eyes glistened.

"You tried the drug?" Steve asked, interested to hear more.

Randolph shook his head, looking thoughtful. "Detective, let me assure you that I have nothing to do with these people. I'm a photographer who does his job and sometimes falls for one of his models. Like you." He stroked Steve's hand suggestively.

Steve pulled his hand away as gently as possible. "Listen, Randolph, I need more information. Where do I find this club? And do you know a name I can connect that group with?"

"Not here," Randolph said, looking around nervously. "I'm scared to say much more."

"So we should meet with Detective Curry as soon as possible at a safe place. Now I have to leave." Steve started out the door, but Randolph grabbed his hand and held him back.

"Oh no, you can't leave me just now. I need someone to take care of me. Enrico left me, and I don't know where to go. Please keep me company tonight."

Steve squeezed Randolph's hand and tried to think of a convenient answer that didn't sound too cruel, when they heard a noise from the hall.

"That must be my partner," Steve said, edging into the corridor.

"You've got a partner? You're engaged to somebody?" Desperately Randolph blocked the door. "Steve, let me hold you. Just one kiss, and I'll let you go." He grabbed Steve around the waist and leaned in close, his mouth only inches from Steve's.

My God what's happening here? Randolph, stop. I don't want anything from you. Steve turned his head to the side to avoid the kiss, but Randolph grabbed Steve's head with a steel grip and turned him until their mouths touched.

"What's going on here?" The door flew open, and a man stood in the doorway. He had black hair combed back from his forehead, and his white shirt was half-open.

"Enrico! I—I didn't know you were here. Where have you been?" Randolph abruptly let go of Steve, staring at the other man, mesmerized.

"Away on business," Enrico said in an icy tone. "I see you're amusing yourself pretty well without me."

Steve took advantage of the argument and rushed past the two men.

"Steve, listen! There's a party at the club next weekend," Randolph cried. "I can tell you things you never—"

Steve heard Randolph shout after him, but he didn't care, he only wanted to be out of there.

Chapter Two

STEVE RAN out of the building, welcoming the cool air on his flushed cheeks. He took a deep breath. It was finally over!

He wiped his face, realizing that his hand was trembling. Belatedly, shock set in. Randolph had almost kissed him! Thanks to Enrico, he had managed to get away just in time.

Where was Bob? He was nowhere to be seen. Steve glanced up and down the dark road. There was only a little traffic and very few people on the street.

Damn, Bob, where are you? Steve felt uncomfortable in his clothes—they stuck on his skin because of the body oil. He shivered, thinking about Randolph's advances.

This neighborhood looked unfamiliar, so he decided to find a taxi to get home. The tooting of a car horn behind him made him jerk.

"Bob! Where have you been?" Steve was overjoyed and angry at the same time. Bob sat there, grinning apologetically behind the wheel of his Mercedes. Steve yanked the passenger-side door open and slid into the car.

"Sorry for being late, but after I took Linda home, I got stuck in traffic. Should have taken the highway." Bob looked at Steve as if Steve had grown two heads. "My God, what happened to you?"

"What d'you mean?"

"Your hair. You look like a—" Bob paused. "You look like a Latin lover, with 'dippity-do' everywhere." A mischievous smile lit his face. "I guess the shoot went well."

"Don't ask! Take me home. I need a shower and a bit of normalcy." Steve touched his hair, disgusted.

Bob frowned. "Everything okay, partner? You look stressed."

"Just get me home. Oh, but let's stop and get something edible." Steve pointed at a Mexican diner at the next corner.

LOADED WITH two bags of food and a six-pack, they stumbled up the stairs to Steve's apartment.

"Now, what happened?" Bob asked, putting the food on the kitchen counter and opening two beers.

"Just a minute. Have to get that oil off my body. Be right back." Steve disappeared hurriedly into the bathroom. He adjusted the water temperature in the shower and shed his clothes.

He started to lock the door against intrusion but stopped himself. The memories of Randolph hovering outside the dressing room were still fresh. Here at home, though, Steve should feel safe. He shook himself to get rid of the lingering fear.

He knew he had to tell Bob about the strange situation. Self-conscious, Steve left the door ajar to prove to himself that he hadn't changed because of the way Randolph had treated him.

"Fuck!" Steve tried to wash the gel out of his hair, but one application of shampoo didn't do the trick. The sticky product seemed to have bonded with his hair. It must be some kind of unusual gel especially for models. He poured more shampoo on his hands and lathered his hair again. Even after rinsing with lots of water, his hair still felt sticky and not at all clean.

"You need any help there?" Bob asked from the living room. There was a smile in his voice.

"Why should I? You said you liked me looking like a Latin lover," Steve said from under the spray of water.

"Can't hear you. Wait…. What's the problem?"

The shower curtain moved, and Bob peeked around the edge.

"I can't get rid of this gel. Any ideas?" Water droplets trailed down Steve's face. He was desperate.

Bob laughed. "Hmm, what about dish soap? I remember when I was a boy I used the stuff. I hated that damn pomade I had to put on every Sunday and washed it out as soon as possible." Bob left the room.

Steve continued to scrub with more shampoo. The water cooled and he began to get cold. *What if nothing helps?*

"Here we go," Bob said confidently. He turned the shower off and leaned in, holding a green bottle. "Bow your head so I can lather your hair."

Steve felt Bob's hands rub the liquid in his hair. The thought that someone he knew so well was touching him felt really good.

"I think you'll be fine," Bob said, sounding content. "Rinse it out well."

Steve grabbed the shower nozzle. "Thanks." He was aware he was naked in front of Bob, but unlike with Randolph, Steve didn't feel awkward at all. It felt so good to have a friend he could share intimate things with.

"Your beer is getting warm. Hurry up." Bob grabbed a towel and put it on the rack before he left the room.

"In a minute," Steve muttered under the spray of water. He turned off the shower, draped the towel around his waist, and trotted into the bedroom to get dressed in fresh clothes.

"I'M FULL... and beat." Steve wiped the corners of his mouth with two fingers and leaned back against the couch cushions. "Bob, that guy Randolph is crazy. I mean, he isn't a freak, but he really thought I would fall for him. He had to put some oil on my body for the camera, and he touched me... look, like this." Steve put his hands on Bob's chest, imitating Randolph.

"So what? I like it." Bob smiled in mock ecstasy.

"Yeah, now it sounds funny, but when I was alone with Randolph, I didn't know what he was up to. After he took the pictures, he was willing to give me the information," Steve said, still going over the encounter in his head. "He told me about a club where members have access to these new drugs but said he had nothing to do with it. When I told him I had to leave and said my partner was going to pick me up, he misinterpreted and thought I was involved with you!" Steve's voice started to rise as he remembered what had happened. "He blocked the door and didn't let me go."

"What did he do?" Bob frowned and put his hand on Steve's arm. "Did he hurt you?"

"No, but he put his arms around my waist and tried to kiss me."

"Son of a bitch," Bob hissed, moving his hand up to Steve's shoulder. He met Steve's eyes with a worried expression.

"He wanted me to spend the night with him because he's been lonely since Enrico left him. And then, speak of the devil, Enrico showed up just in time." Steve sighed, sipping from his beer.

"Enrico must be having second thoughts and wanted to get back together with him," Bob said.

"Yes, he was enraged at seeing Randolph with me. I took the chance and left instead of getting caught up in that mess." Steve leaned back, relaxing for the first time. "I can't tell you how glad I am to be home. Never talk me into something like that again, buddy."

Bob exhaled audibly. "If I had known.... I'm sorry. So much for doing a favor for that guy and the possibility of a new snitch. Who knows what his information is worth?" He shrugged with a frown. "We'll have a talk with him again. Maybe tomorrow after our shift," Bob proposed and then emptied his can of beer.

Steve nodded and stifled a yawn. "Okay, let's call it a day. You wanna crash here tonight?"

"After your experience with Randolph, you still want to spend the night with a guy?" Bob teased.

"Yeah, let me think it over." Steve pretended to consider. "I'm glad to have you here, buddy. I'll take the couch, if you want. My bed is surely more comfortable for your back."

"No way, Steve." Bob got up and went to the drawer to get the extra linen. With his arms loaded with sheets and blankets, he smiled at Steve. "Your couch has my name on it. It's okay. In case you have nightmares about photographers, just call me, I'm right here."

Steve looked at him. It was as if he were seeing Bob for the first time. This tall guy, his silky hair gleaming in the lamplight, was his best friend. He was a tough cop, showing no mercy when needed. Steve loved how Bob's expression could turn instantly from anger to joy, as it did after they'd had a successful bust. And Bob had the kind of beauty a lot of women fell for, with his strong, muscular legs that didn't seem to end, his smooth chest, and soft smile.

Today, although he'd been late picking Steve up, it hadn't been his fault. Steve grinned, imagining himself one of Bob's charity cases.

"Stop grinning, and help me here." Bob threw the extra blanket in Steve's direction and laughed when it covered Steve's upper body.

"I'll teach you how to treat the owner of this place with respect." Steve took a step, not realizing the coffee table was so near. He bumped his shin right into the corner.

"Shit! I think I've broken my knee," he yelled, tossing the blanket away to examine his shin. Seeing the concern on Bob's face, he hurried to put his whining into perspective. "It's not too bad. The coffee table was in the way."

"And you call me clumsy! You don't even know where your furniture is?"

"Shuddup. Go to bed," Steve interrupted with a laugh. "I'll see you in the morning. If you're up earlier than me, you can make breakfast." He frowned, trying to remember the last time he'd gone grocery shopping. "There must be something in the fridge." With a light pat on Bob's stomach, he walked past him into the bedroom.

Steve left the door ajar, just in case they needed to talk. He heard Bob rummaging, making the bed on the couch, and then silence. Content, Steve turned onto his side. He was almost asleep when he heard Bob in the living room.

"Steve?" Bob called out. "I've got something on my mind. Linda is a beautiful woman." Bob paused and sighed. "I got the feeling she wouldn't have objected if I'd spent the night with her."

"So what held you back?" Steve asked, turning over again.

"You, dummy." Bob gave a short laugh. "Remember? I promised to pick you up. And I arrived too late to save you from that lonely photographer."

Steve felt remorseful. He had spoiled Bob's date with a beautiful woman, all because he'd expected Bob to pick him up. Hesitantly, he asked, "Would you have liked to keep Linda company? You could have called and told me to take a cab home. Instead you end up spending another evening with me."

Steve heard Bob chuckle. "I wasn't in the mood to get laid. Something was missing." He sounded pensive. "Aw, I think I'm getting old. What about you? Any cute ladies driving you crazy lately?"

Steve didn't answer right away. He stared up at the dark ceiling and saw his own blurry reflection in the mirror on the ceiling, and the empty space beside him. It hit him that it had been a while since he'd had a woman in his bed. Was it time to get more active? Or was Bob right and they were getting old?

He cleared his throat. "It's the job, don't you think? Double shifts and working at night doesn't do a lot to improve my sex life." He heard the old couch creak when Bob moved.

After a huge yawn, Bob said, "Yeah, there's an idea. We need to ask Lieutenant Rollins for some days off to take care of our special personal needs. Then we can hit the road to chat up some hot ladies." There was a smile in his voice.

Steve watched himself in the mirror and imagined a woman lying by his side.

"Sounds like a plan, buddy. Nighty-night," Steve murmured, closing his eyes. His imagination ran free with fantasies of half-naked women writhing in ecstasy.

"G'night, pal," Bob said.

The silence was protective and familiar.

Steve followed his erotic thoughts drowsily. The women were getting more curvaceous, and Steve let his hand wander south, touching the erotic spot just below his navel. He shivered, and his cock responded to the touch of his hand. He ran his fingers over the soft skin below the waistband of his pajamas.

Not wanting Bob to hear him, Steve tried to breathe normally. He smiled, wondering if Bob would guess what he was doing from the sounds alone. But Bob would understand. It wasn't the first time this had happened when they were together. They were so familiar with each other, there had been many other times when they'd slept in adjoining rooms and Steve had heard Bob giving himself pleasure. It had never bothered him.

Steve took hold of his cock and teased the flesh, running his hand along the shaft. It had been a long time since he'd masturbated, and he had missed the wonderful sensation. Exhausted by the job, he hadn't given in to bodily pleasures enough. He squeezed with increasing intensity and fondled the hardening flesh. Breathing heavily, he watched his reflection in the dark mirror. Steve tried recalling the images of naked women, but they no longer came to mind. He was still hard and getting frustrated. Another image came to him as he ran his hand up and down his length. A tall figure with legs that didn't seem to end, a smile he could drown in—

My God, it's Bob!

Steve stilled his hand, too puzzled to go on. He was attracted to Bob?

The ache of his cock urged him to continue and, giving in, Steve delved into memories of Bob. He saw the smooth chest, the fine hair on the muscular thighs, and the best thing—the prominent cock between Bob's legs. Steve gasped with desire.

They had touched each other accidentally plenty of times, and he had never thought a thing about it. It was just Bob. They stood close together every single day, patted each other's bellies, and he'd never gotten hard before.

The affection that had always existed between them seemed to turn into something exciting and new. Steve fondled and squeezed his balls, feeling the vibration that signaled his orgasm. With the image of Bob undressing to reveal his fully erect penis, Steve came.

He held back a little cry, afraid to wake Bob. Trembling, he released his cock, running his hand over his sweaty chest. His nipples were still hard, so he stroked them briefly as he caught his breath. Warm stickiness between his thighs. He grabbed a part of the bedsheet to clean himself.

Steve lay, sated, listening for noises from the living room, but all was still. Steve turned on his side, too tired to think about what had happened. He fell asleep.

"HEY, YOU, the next time you want me to make breakfast, make sure there is something edible in your kitchen. A half-empty bag of donuts doesn't count, and neither does the cheese that seems to have developed a life of its own." Bob shook his head in disbelief, steering the Mercedes around the next corner.

"I haven't been to the grocery store because we were on the road the last few days with the investigation and chasing that crazy guy who was stalking your friend Linda." Steve pushed his sunglasses on. "Breakfast is on me," he said, fumbling for his wallet. He pointed to a diner on the corner. "Stop at Dinah's over there. They make the best scrambled eggs, and I'm starving."

Steve's mouth watered as he imagined a full breakfast. Randolph was still on his mind like a bad dream, and he needed to get rid of all the unpleasant memories.

Bob pulled into the parking lot of the restaurant and looked for an empty space. "Wonder why it's so full at this time of the day?" he asked and whistled when he saw a car leaving a parking spot. "Here we go."

Bob maneuvered the car into the empty space and gave a sigh of relief.

"I know why it's so crowded," Steve said and pointed to a sign above the entrance.

Breakfast half price!

"I'm not that hungry," Bob said, sounding moody, as they walked to the front door.

The place was packed, and a babble of voices spilled from the overcrowded restaurant. It would take a long time to get a table. Steve glanced at Bob, trying to decide whether to stay or leave right away.

"Steve? Bob? Wait!" A dark-skinned young woman made her way to the door, beaming at them.

"Bella? Is it you?" Steve couldn't believe his eyes. Bella had been a waitress at Larry's pub. It stood next to the police department, and he and Bob used to meet there after a shift.

Bob added, "We haven't seen you in a long time. We heard you got married. Are you working here now?" He gave her a quick hug.

"Sure am! I'm running the place with my hubby, and today is the reopening." Bella looked around the crowded place, searching for an empty table.

"That's fantastic news!" Steve said sincerely. "Couldn't happen to a nicer woman."

"I have a quiet table over there. It's reserved for personal friends." Bella smiled and led them to a section in the back. "Take a seat. You're invited to have breakfast on the house. Freddie and I bought the franchise on this place. We hope it's going to be successful." She took out a writing pad. "Now, what can I bring you? The bacon and eggs are beyond compare." She pulled out her pencil, ready to take the order.

"I'm not that hungry," Bob said. "First of all, congratulations. You deserve your own restaurant." Bob slid into the booth next to Steve.

Steve leafed through the menu. "Two Special Breakfasts," he ordered, completely ignoring Bob's weak protests.

"Okay, and coffee, with a lot of sugar for you, Steve." Bella scribbled the order down and left.

"How does she know I love my coffee with lots of sugar?" Steve asked.

"You have to ask? You pestered her every time we were at Larry's and always complained when she forgot the sugar." Bob smirked, elbowing Steve playfully.

"Yeah, she must know us pretty well to remember our eating habits. For you only the healthy stuff." Steve wrinkled his nose. "Anyway. We have a long shift ahead and need a real breakfast." He leaned back, getting comfortable on the bench.

Bob played with his knife and fork pensively. "I'd like to question Randolph about that club he told you about. With Randolph's help, we might have a lead on this case."

"At least everything that happened yesterday could turn out to be useful after all." Steve sighed.

"Here we go." Bella carried over their breakfast plates, setting one in front of each of them. "Enjoy your meal!" She gave them a bright smile and hurried off to another customer.

"That's what your little heart desired, right?" Bob said, looking at the plates loaded with sausages, toast, eggs, and hash browns.

"Who knows when our next decent meal will be?" Steve dug in.

Bob checked his watch. "I'm pretty sure you'll be hungry again before noon."

Steve grunted in response. They ate in silence, enjoying their breakfasts.

"That was good. What's next?" Steve joked, suppressing a belch. He shifted on his seat.

"It's over there." Bob pointed to the restrooms.

"You are so funny. Stay here." Steve put his hand on Bob's shoulder and squeezed gently. "I'll be right back."

"Yes, Mom," Bob joked, waving to another waiter to refill their coffee cups.

On his way to the restroom, Steve passed the door to the kitchen. He took a peek and saw lots of activity inside. There were several cooks and other kitchen helpers whirling around the stoves and counters on such a busy morning. Steve saw a tall man giving orders to the cooks. Was that Bella's husband? Somehow the man looked familiar to him. Steve shook his head, dismissing the thought, and headed to the john.

"Everything okay?" Bob asked when he came back.

"Sure. You need any details?" Steve smiled.

Bob rolled his eyes. "I can think of better things than that. Hey, the place is really filled." He looked around. "And almost all young people."

Steve snorted. "Yes, I feel like a hundred years old. It's a good thing Bella has her own restaurant. What did she say her husband's name was?" He sat down, sipping the steaming coffee.

Bob shrugged. "Why d'you ask? I think she said it's Freddie."

"Well, I might be wrong, but I saw a tall guy in the kitchen who looked familiar. Could be that Freddie who sold drugs to kids. You remember? We busted him a couple of years ago."

Bob frowned. "Yeah, I know who you mean. The guy waited for the kids when school was out, offering them drugs. You think he's Bella's husband?"

"Don't know," Steve answered. He could read Bob's mind and guessed he'd be thinking: *Let's hope Freddie's abandoned his old business.*

To distract himself Steve surveyed the busy place. Every table was occupied with customers chatting and laughing while having breakfast. At the table next to them, four young women were sharing a pot of tea and a plate of toast. Two of them kept glancing in their direction.

Steve nudged Bob. "You see those chicks, buddy? Remember what we were talking about last night? Having some fun with the ladies again." Steve smiled at the girls, and they smiled back before going back to their conversation.

"Which table do you mean? Ah, I see." Bob gave his sweetest smile, but by then two men had walked up to their table and distracted the girls. All four women welcomed the men with loud hellos.

Steve sighed. Maybe next time.

Bob yawned broadly, then said, "A breakfast like this makes me tired, I could grab a few zees." He stretched lazily, closing his eyes for a moment.

Steve couldn't help looking at his partner's lean body. The way he stretched so smoothly and relaxed, like a tiger in the jungle, completely secure in his beauty and strength.

"Something wrong with me? Don't tell me I buttoned my shirt wrong again." Bob checked it, stroking his hand over his chest and belly.

"Huh?" Steve gaped and looked away. "Nothing, really." He didn't know what was going on with him. Bob looked so sexy. Something was definitely wrong lately. He cleared his throat. "Everything's all right, pal. Let's hit the road before I get sleepy too."

BOB DROVE the Mercedes, both of them watching the sidewalks for signs of criminal activity, as usual.

A domestic disturbance call broke into their lazy morning ride—a drunken couple yelling obscenities and threatening each other with violence. Steve sprained his thumb overpowering the raging husband while Bob took care of the sobbing wife.

After they arrested the man, they went to assist with a bust at a bar downtown. There had been rumors that the establishment allowed gambling. When they arrived they found the establishment full of people watching a football game on the little TV above the bar. The back room looked tidy, with no evidence that anyone had recently played poker for money.

"I'll bet they had a lookout who alerted them that we were coming," Steve said, sucking on his sore thumb. "I can forget writing my reports with this finger," he complained, looking at Bob with puppy-dog eyes.

"Don't worry. You never use your thumb typing reports," Bob said, ignoring Steve's beg for help. "We're done here. Let's head to the station to do some paperwork."

WHEN THEY arrived at the precinct, Lieutenant George Rollins was scolding Officers Holloway and Bolton for not doing their reports properly. Steve exchanged a meaningful look with Bob and hurried to his desk. Soon they were engrossed in writing their reports.

At one point Bob waggled his fingers at Steve to hand him the half-written report about the altercation between the husband and wife. Steve smiled at him and without thinking blew him a kiss. Bob raised an eyebrow. Steve felt his cheeks flush and hoped Bob didn't notice.

The morning's reports took all afternoon to finish. After printing them out, Bob got up to give them to Rollins. Just as he was about to knock, the door flew open and Rollins rushed into the squad room, bumping into Bob.

"Sorry, Detective. A man walking by found a dead male in the Southgate Park. Curry and Randall, you go and check the crime scene," Rollins said gruffly.

"Sir, we were just about to clock out," Steve protested with a groan.

"Do that later!" Rollins stabbed a finger at him and Bob. "After you send in an initial report, clock out for the night and write up your official accounts in the morning."

Bob stood up, grabbing his jacket with resignation. "Did the first cops on the scene say how the victim died?"

"Medical examiner hadn't gotten there yet. I hope this isn't another drug-related death." Rollins frowned, shaking his head sadly. Drug-related crimes always disturbed their superior. "We've had enough of those in the last few months. I'm fed up with bad news. We have to intensify our efforts to catch those responsible. Not just the pushers, but the dealers and traffickers. Understood?" Rollins looked at them, his eyes glistening with anger and despair.

Steve knew Rollins was thinking of his own kid. His son Greg was in high school, and despite the efforts of the police, every campus in Culver City had drugs. If Greg were offered marijuana—or worse, heroin—would he be tempted? Or had he learned enough of the dangers from his father's work?

"Rollins is on the edge," Bob said when the older man had walked back into his office. "You coming?"

Steve nodded, following him down the hall to the elevator. "By the way, we should pay the photo studio a visit and interview Randolph. I hope he's still there, but like us, photographers don't have regular work hours." Steve pushed the down button repeatedly. "Shit! The damn thing's stuck again. Let's take the stairs."

Before Bob could respond, Steve had reached the staircase and hurried down. "What's the rush?" Bob asked.

"Dunno, just a feeling we might be too late."

"The man at Southgate is already dead. Take your time," Bob reassured his partner, but Steve didn't slow down.

"Tell me again what Randolph said about the place where the new drug is originating. What was it called?" Bob wanted to know.

Once downstairs, Steve paused. "Randolph thinks the drugs are coming out of an exclusive club called Steps to Heaven. Do you know where it is?"

Bob frowned. "Could be that place on Seventh." He shrugged.

Steve got into his black Thunderbird. The car didn't look bad, but it had its issues, and Bob yanked at the passenger door twice before he could open it. "Shit! Your damn car needs its door adjusted," Bob complained and slid into the seat.

Steve pulled sharply out of the police garage, tires screeching. He mumbled, "Yeah, my old lady feels that you don't really like her."

Bob snorted. They rode in silence until they got to Southgate Park. A black-and-white and the crime lab van were blocking the entrance. Steve parked haphazardly behind the other two vehicles. A broad path led into the park. Only a few rays of the late-afternoon sun found their way through the tall trees along the path. The undergrowth was in darkness. Steve turned up the collar of his leather jacket. "It's cooled down."

"Look, our people are over there!" Bob pointed to the left. A narrow path disappeared between some bushes. Men in protective gear were examining the ground.

"Hey, Jenkins, what have you found?" Bob approached a middle-aged man crouching near a bush.

"Hi, Curry. Seems like I saw you just the other day over a body like this one," the older man said with a tired smile. "It's the ninth death in a short time, but, it's not drug abuse. The man is lying under a bush. At first we thought it might be a possible suicide. Except it's obvious that the shot was fired from a short distance away." The coroner indicated the angle the shot came from. "We haven't found the weapon so far." He carefully placed some dirt inside an evidence bag. "Have a look at him. The body is over there, covered with a tarp, but we didn't touch a thing."

"So homicide, not suicide. Thanks, Jenkins," Bob said.

Steve was already on his way to the body. He bent down and lifted the tarp to look at the dead man. He couldn't believe his eyes.

"Oh, my God," he gasped. "Bob, come here! It's Randolph, the photographer." Steve shuddered, memories of the night before very fresh. "That's horrible."

Bob crouched next to him. "Yes, it's him." Bob grimaced. "Damn, there goes our informant. You last saw him at what time yesterday?"

Steve put the tarp back over the dead body. "I left the studio about 7:00 p.m. Enrico was angry when he showed up, but it seemed that the two lovebirds would make up. Shit." Steve wondered if he could have prevented the murder if he'd stayed longer.

Bob stood up and looked at his watch. "So it's been twenty-three hours since you saw him."

"Jenkins," Bob called out. "This is Randolph Foreman. He's a fashion photographer. We were at his studio last night."

"Good. Thanks, guys." Jenkins wrote out a toe tag and motioned to the morgue crew just pulling up to bag the corpse.

"Was there more than one bullet wound?" Steve asked.

Jenkins shook his head. "No, there's only one. And it looks as if the corpse was dragged into the bushes."

"So the man wasn't killed right here," Bob mused.

"Can you tell us the time of death?" Steve wanted to know.

Jenkins made a vague gesture. "Probably between midnight and 4:00 a.m."

"Thanks, Jenkins," Steve said, feeling relieved. At that time he had been at home with Bob, so they couldn't suspect him.

"You coming? It's past six." Bob yawned, rubbing his eyes. "Let's call it a day."

Steve nodded. "Rollins said we could finish up in the morning." Looking at the dead body he said, "At least Randolph was able to give me a starting point about Blue Rocket. We need to put an APB out on Enrico, to get his side of the story."

"He's definitely a person of interest here," Bob agreed. Hands shoved in their pockets, they walked back to the park entrance, lost in thought. A young uniformed cop leaned on his police car at the roadside. He waved at Bob and Steve. "I'm on duty. Can I help you? Is it a suicide?"

Bob stepped nearer. "Officer, send a unit to the Fashion Photos studio at Morgan Avenue, corner of Tenth Street, and seal the door. It's a possible crime scene."

"Yes, sir!" The young officer snapped a salute that made Steve wonder if he'd ever been that eager.

This added another dimension to an already complicated case. Was Randolph's murder connected to Steps to Heaven? Or was it a coincidence that he had given Steve info about the new drug right before he died?

Steve dropped Bob back at the police station to pick up his car. "See you," they said in unison, and Steve smiled. Bob made the victory sign and disappeared into the police garage.

Steve had a dreamless night. At least, he didn't remember any when he woke up the next morning. Stretching, he thought about finding Randolph's body in the park. Had he been the last person to see Randolph before he was murdered? Had Enrico killed his lover? And what was Randolph's connection to Steps to Heaven?

Chapter Three

STEVE HAD just pulled on his jeans when there was a knock on the door.

"Is that you, Bob?" he asked, putting on his wristwatch, a new Yamamoto with many special functions he still hadn't completely figured out.

"Who else?" Bob answered.

Steve opened the door to let him in. "Hey, you. I woke up this morning thinking about Randolph," Steve said, rubbing his eyes.

"And suddenly it hit you that he's dead. I know how you feel." Bob laid a comforting hand on Steve's arm. "Here, I brought bagels and cream cheese in case you're hungry." He went into the kitchen and put the bag on the counter.

"Yeah, let's have breakfast. I'll make coffee." Steve was glad Bob was thinking along the same lines as he was. They often reacted the same way, although they were so different in character and behavior.

"Sorry, I didn't have any old congealing pizza for you this morning, and no root beer," Bob teased.

"Bagels are fine, thanks." Steve filled their cups with coffee. He always felt better with Bob around. Steve was confident they would uncover some clues to Randolph's death and get to work on the drug case too.

Putting cream cheese on his bagel, Bob said, "I've been thinking. I should question the other employees at Fashion Photos. Maybe they'll be able to shed some light on Randolph's relationship with Enrico."

"Nobody else was there when I left except Randolph and Enrico," Steve put in.

Bob took a bite of his bagel and ate with pleasure. He swallowed and said, "And I'd like to have a talk with the owner of the studio and some of the other photographers and models."

"You sound as if you plan to do this on your own. Are you worried I'm too involved to work the investigation?" Steve asked.

"Of course not, buddy," Bob said. He sipped his hot coffee. "I can question Enrico alone because he won't recognize me. You stay out of that interrogation because we don't want to compromise his statement. You were there shortly before Randolph died." He looked at Steve and added, "You and I need to admit to Rollins that we knew Randolph through Linda. And you should tell him about the photo shoot."

"If I'm considered a suspect in this case, I may not be allowed to be in on the investigation at all," Steve said sourly. He got up and put his plate in the sink. "We need to know the exact time of death. Good thing you crashed at my place, huh? At least I've got an alibi!"

"Calm down." Bob looked at Steve, sending warmth and confidence. "At the risk of sounding cruel, you'll be asked about your relationship with Randolph. Enrico saw you there."

"Shit!" Steve paced around the kitchen until Bob got up and grabbed Steve's arms from behind to calm him down.

"When you get ballistics and other evidence from the crime lab, we can meet for lunch—let's say at Dinah's—to decide what to do next. Okay?" Bob put his hands on Steve's shoulders and started a light massage. "I really prefer having you in an interrogation with me."

Steve leaned back into Bob's solid presence and nodded.

ONE HOUR later Steve was sitting in their office, sorting through the evidence and reports he had on Randolph's death. The photographer had been shot with a .38, probably a Colt, not far from the place he had been found.

Steve sat, head in his hands, thinking. He hated being in this situation. He was too closely involved, meeting Randolph one day before he was murdered. What could be the reason for the crime? Who would have a reason to kill the photographer?

Steve thought about Enrico. He had been so furious seeing Randolph with another man. Randolph had mentioned a meeting with his boss he didn't plan to attend. And then there was the other guy, Chris, who had reminded Randolph of the date with a man called Sanders. What about any other relationships Randolph might have had? Maybe another disappointed lover or a girl who wanted more than he was willing to give—

"Steve and Bob! In my office!" Rollins's voice startled Steve out of his funk.

Steve had known this moment would come, and he wasn't sure how much he should tell their captain about the photo shoot.

"Take a seat." Rollins looked at a big folder in front of him, leafing through the pages as if searching for a detail he hadn't seen before. He looked up at Steve. "You and Bob were the first detectives on the scene of this Randolph Foreman, so it's yours. Tell me, where's your partner?" Frowning, Rollins glanced around the room as if he expected Bob to be hidden somewhere.

"Lieutenant, Bob is already at the photo studio, asking the employees about Randolph's death." Steve rubbed his hands and squirmed in his seat.

"Why aren't you with your partner?" Rollins asked as if his patience was wearing thin.

Steve took a deep breath and looked at his superior. "Well, Bob thought it would be better if he did the interrogation alone. Enrico, Randolph's previous model, saw me when I was at the photo studio—"

"Randall, speak clearly, or I'll send you back to the academy for a refresher course on presenting evidence!" Rollins dropped his hand onto the folder, crumpling some papers in the process.

Steve plucked up his courage and explained that he had met Randolph on Tuesday at Linda Thornton's photo shoot. "Randolph promised to give us some information about the drug deaths. He has—I mean, he had connections to a club where models and artists were using the new drug, Blue Rocket." Steve took a slow breath. "Bob and I were going to go over and ask him about it today. Now it's too late, and I wanna know who killed him." Steve gestured back at the squad room where he'd left the case file. He hesitated, not sure if he should tell his boss about his short involvement as a model.

"Anything else I should know?" Rollins's gaze lingered on Steve's face. The concern Steve saw in Rollins's eyes made it easier to admit to posing as a model for the new summer swimwear collection.

"You posed in swim trunks for this guy?" Rollins asked seriously—but there was a hint of amusement in his eyes. "Thank you for telling me. Write out an official statement of your career"—he chuckled—"and the altercation with this Enrico. Then go find that partner of yours and find out all you can on that club. What's the name of it?"

"Steps to Heaven."

Rollins pointed at the bio sheet on the murdered man. "We need to know everything about this Randolph Foreman. I want to have your reports as soon as possible. Get outta here, and do your job! And no unauthorized actions! Understood?"

Steve nodded, relieved that Rollins hadn't made fun of his brief modeling career. "Thanks," he said, making his way out of the office.

He needed to find more information about the Steps to Heaven club.

FROM THE outside the photography studio had nothing fancy to offer. It was an old building with three stories, and the gray walls needed a coat of paint. The neighborhood didn't look any better: bleak office buildings and a wholesaler of leather clothing lined the street. Bob walked into the foyer of the studio. What a contrast! Spotlights illuminated giant photos of celebrities from the film and fashion business. Some models posed in seductive lingerie, looking invitingly at the observer. Fascinated, Bob stared at the walls.

His thoughts went to his old classmate, and he wondered if she had heard about Randolph's death. She had told him she planned to visit with her mother in Philadelphia, so it was possible she hadn't gotten the news. He should have a talk with her too. Maybe she could give them more information.

"Can I help you?" A voice from the right interrupted Bob's thoughts. A man was sitting behind a black desk, in conversation with a lady in high heels. With her stylish air and clothes, Bob assumed that she was a model like Linda Thornton.

Bob cleared his throat. He read the man's name tag. "Yes, indeed, Mr. Rivers." Bob took out his badge and showed it to the man. "I want to speak with Mr. John Sanders, the owner of the studio. My name is Bob Curry, CCPD. We're investigating the death of one of your photographers."

"The police were here this morning going through Mr. Foreman's office. How awful!" Rivers exclaimed. "How can we get any work done?" He bit his lip, obviously distressed. Bob wasn't sure if it was because of the death or the lack of work. "Randolph was one of our best. The cops earlier wouldn't tell us anything, just that he was dead. The guy had his way with some of his models. He had quite a reputation...." Rivers shook his head, stopping in midsentence.

"Yeah? Go on," Bob coaxed, hoping to hear some more details.

"The poor guy, he often put up with the wrong people, if you know what I mean," Rivers said in a confidential tone. "He fell in love and didn't want to let go, and that caused problems. But that's none of my business. I'll call Mr. Sanders. You can take a seat in the lounge to wait for him." He pointed to a niche in the background. An ostentatious red plush sofa invited the visitor.

Bob had just sat down when a door on the other side of the entrance hall opened and a man in a tailored gray suit emerged. He looked around as if searching for someone. Bob met his gaze and got up. "Mr. Sanders? I'm Bob Curry, CCPD." Bob showed his badge again. "I have some questions."

Sanders pointed along the hall. "Please, follow me to my office, Mr. Burry."

"Curry," Bob corrected dryly.

Sanders smiled sourly and led Bob to his office on the left. The small room looked overloaded with many pictures of models of both genders, posing in different outfits. Some of them looked out of date, probably former celebrities. Bob recognized Linda Thornton's photo.

"Have a seat." Sanders pointed to a brown leather armchair in front of a small desk.

Bob sat on the edge of the chair, wishing he had Steve's Yamamoto watch to check the time.

"You smoke? Sanders offered Bob a pack of cigarettes, fumbling in his pocket, presumably for a lighter.

"No, thanks. I'd like to ask you some questions about your employee, Mr. Randolph Foreman. He died yesterday."

"I know. What a tragedy. One of our best photographers." Sanders sighed, obviously concerned. He walked around his desk and sat down in an office chair.

"What can you tell me about Randolph Foreman?" Bob asked, opening his notebook to jot down the man's words.

Lost in thought, Sanders lit a cigarette, inhaling deeply. It was as if he had to think about the right answer to give. Finally he said, "I was always afraid Randy would end up this way. Not that I thought badly about him, he just got into difficulties time and time again. Did he commit suicide?" Sanders looked out of the window with a sad expression. "Once he said, 'I can't go on this way.' Too sad indeed." Sanders shrugged.

"He was killed," Bob stated, watching Sanders's reaction.

"No, that's impossible!" Abruptly Sanders stood up. "Randolph was such a nice guy, and when he was happy, he was so charming. Why would someone kill that innocent man? We all loved him—except his former lovers, maybe." Sanders frowned.

"That's interesting." Bob straightened. "Why would they want to kill him, and who were his lovers?"

Sanders laughed. He sounded like a little barking dog. "Detective, don't expect me to be that well informed." He dragged on his cigarette. "I can't tell you details, but rumors said Randolph easily fell in love with his models." He shrugged.

"We need a list of the men Randolph has worked with in the last six months," Bob said.

Sanders raised his eyebrows. "That'll be a lot of work. Randolph was a busy man. Wait!" Sanders stubbed out his cigarette. "His recent model is Enrico Gonzales. Possible that they had an affair."

Bob scribbled down Sanders's comments in his notebook. "Enrico Gonzales was supposed to show up for a photo session and didn't come. Randolph was quite put out about the matter."

Sanders lit another cigarette. "I spoke to him this morning." Sanders smoked for a moment. "He told me that Randolph was with another man on Tuesday night. Enrico wasn't happy, I can tell you. But he would never be able to hurt his lover, in case they were involved with each other." Sanders stubbed out his cigarette into an overflowing ashtray.

"So you think Enrico isn't the jealous type who would seek revenge after finding his lover with another man?" Bob asked.

"Oh, Enrico is a hothead. But I can't believe he would do such a cruel thing." Sanders stood up. "Detective, that's all I can tell you. I have a lunch date with one of my new models. Business must go on, you know." He smiled apologetically and gestured at the door.

"One more question." Bob started a new line in his notebook. "Have you got Mr. Gonzales's address? And where were you between Tuesday night and Wednesday morning?"

"That's two questions already, Officer." Sanders's smile was forced. He walked around the desk to show that the conversation was over.

"So?" Bob leaned back without getting out of his chair, pretending he was fully relaxed.

Sanders paced from the desk to the door.

"Am I a suspect now? On Tuesday evening I had a meeting with my assistant Chris Barber, and we were waiting for Randolph Foreman, who didn't show up. Later that evening I met with my girlfriend, and she stayed with me all night." He bristled, obviously annoyed at the questions. "About yesterday... let me check my calendar." Sanders returned to the desk to flip through his book. "Here it is: Wednesday, appointment with Dr. Glassman in Santa Barbara. My girl and I got stuck in a traffic jam on Canyon Drive and arrived late." He crossed his arms, glaring at Bob. "You can get Enrico's address at the front desk. You'll excuse me now." Sanders hurried to the door and opened it. He bumped into a man who looked familiar to Bob.

"Chris, I know we have to hurry. I'll be ready in a minute." Sanders motioned Chris outside, and they were about to leave.

Bob stood, flipped his notebook closed, and called Chris back. "Mr. Barber, I presume? I want to talk to you too."

Chris looked at Sanders, who rolled his eyes indignantly.

"What's the matter, man?" Chris asked, still standing in the doorframe, strands of dark hair falling over his forehead and hiding his eyes.

"Would you mind coming in?" Bob pointed at the desk. "Mr. Sanders, I'd like to meet with him privately for a few minutes, if we could use your office?"

"As if I have a choice in the matter!" Sanders growled. "I'll be calling my lawyer."

Hesitantly Chris walked in, his hands deep in his pockets.

"What was your relationship with Randolph Foreman?" Bob asked, perching on the armchair next to the desk.

"None of your business. And if you're from the press, you can lift your ass outta here. We're fed up with nosy reporters like you!"

"Whoa, not so fast. I'm Detective Curry from CCPD." Bob held up his badge. "Please take a seat. And shut the door behind you." Bob forced himself to stay calm. He would be late for his lunch break with Steve at this rate.

"I don't know anything about Randy, except that he was crazy about the models he worked with. Weren't you here Tuesday with another man?" Chris eyed Bob suspiciously.

"I'm asking the questions here," Bob stated dryly. "So, you were telling me about Randolph's relationships with the models?"

Chris shrugged. "Randy seemed to have the hots for the man he was with on Tuesday. Don't tell me, that guy is—was involved with Randy? You think he's got something to do with Randy's death?" He looked at Bob. "I can give you a description of him. Dark hair, good-looking…." Chris had a dreamy expression, like a little boy who still believed in fairy tales.

"Tell me what you did two days ago," Bob interrupted. "On Tuesday night you left for the meeting with your boss," Bob reminded Chris, to keep him on track. "What was that meeting about? Why was Randolph needed there?"

Chris looked down. "We planned to expand the business to the East Coast and needed Randy's connections over there. Without him, we'll have to start over from the beginning. Shit."

Bob got up, stashing his notebook in his jacket pocket. "Chris, you're required to answer some more questions at the precinct. Please come over on Monday at nine. Understood?"

Chris nodded hastily and retreated to the door. Together Chris and Bob left the office. Bob went over to the front desk to get Enrico's and Randolph's addresses from the receptionist.

Chapter Four

BOB WALKED into Dinah's Diner, relieved that it wasn't too crowded. He looked around but couldn't spot Steve. Bella was behind the counter. She waved him over to the left, pointing at the corner booth. Bob smiled and made his way past the long buffet.

Steve was sitting with a young woman, chatting, munching on appetizers, and laughing. Bob slowed down as a sharp sting pierced his heart. All of a sudden, he felt abandoned and lonely.

"Hey, Bob. Finally! I thought you'd never come!" Steve waved at him. He scooted over to give Bob enough space to sit down next to him.

Bob squashed in beside Steve and arranged his long legs under the table. "Sorry," he mumbled when he bumped against something.

"Never mind." The woman smiled. She had long blackish hair, dark eyes, and a creamy brown complexion.

Steve beamed at Bob, nudging him in the side. "Bob, this is Jessica, one of the waitresses here. She helped me kill the time. I got some information about the club we're looking for. But now I need a real meal. I'll take a burrito. What about you? A tofu burger?"

Jessica made a face. Covering Bob's hand with his own, Steve said, "Opposites attract, right?"

Bob savored the warmth of Steve's hand on his own, wondering that he felt so much better than a moment before.

Jessica looked at their joined hands and smiled. "Well, Steps to Heaven would be a good place for you guys to hang around. You could meet a lot of people who want a career as a model or an actor. And boys like you are well accepted there too."

Steve took his hand away from Bob's and frowned. "What do you mean by that?"

"Sorry if I came to the wrong conclusion, but you look like you belong together. And that's fine with me." She looked from Steve to Bob and back.

"But we're not—" Bob's elbow in his side stopped him.

Jessica leaned forward, speaking in a confidential voice. "Some of my best friends are gay. At the club you'll feel comfortable and at home. Next Saturday there's a party, and if you'd like to join the fun, I can invite you. New people only get in on the recommendation of a member. Is it a deal?" She beamed at them.

Bob thought quickly. Jessica needn't know they were cops. Hopefully Steve hadn't mentioned it. He nudged Steve with his thigh, and Steve returned the pressure.

"Well, why not?" Bob decided to play along and let Jessica think they were boyfriends. He put his arm around Steve's shoulder and felt Steve tense for a moment. Their eyes locked, and Bob knew that Steve understood the game.

"That would be nice, sweetheart," Steve told Jessica. Without asking, he poked inside Bob's jacket to find a pencil and the notebook. "Tell me your full name?"

"Jessica Parker." She giggled. "My phone number is 555-6752, and you obviously know where I work if you need to get ahold of me quick."

Steve scribbled that down with a side glance at Bob. "And what's the address of Steps to Heaven?"

"On the corner of Winchester and Seventh."

"Okay, we'll be there." Steve finished his notes. "What time?"

"Nine would be fine. I'll be waiting at the entrance." Jessica winked. "But don't be too late, otherwise I'll be inside. They play fantastic music there, and the DJ is so funny." She checked her watch and sighed. "Sorry, boys, but I have to hurry. My lunch break was over fifteen minutes ago. Back to work. See you next Saturday, okay?" She rushed toward the exit, then stopped briefly to wave back at them.

"Bob, why the hell didn't you object when she thought we were gay?" Steve exploded, smacking the table. "We'll never get laid if we act like a couple! I thought I'd have a chance with her...."

"Don't you get it? If we want to find out what's going on in the club, we need to pretend to be one of those wannabe artists," Bob said, checking the menu.

Steve stared at the wall silently.

"I'm in the mood for a big pizza—but not the spicy one," Bob announced.

Steve stared at him in astonishment. "I don't get it. You're scarin' me here. What's going on in that head of yours? You're copying my eating habits and want to go undercover to that club?"

"Have to mix things up a little."

Steve put the menu away. "I'm not hungry anymore."

"Come on, Steve! Going to Steps to Heaven makes sense. It's a way to get closer to the organization spreading Blue Rocket," Bob replied and waved over a waitress to take their order.

"WHAT NOW?" Steve asked, wiping his mouth. He hadn't been at all hungry after Jessica left the table, but once he smelled the enticing aroma of Bob's pizza *al funghi*, he'd helped himself to some.

He'd really hoped to score with the pretty waitress. He'd been so horny lately, and images of a naked Bob weren't helping matters. What he needed was a pretty lady in his bed to fill the emptiness of the last few months. But from that moment when he'd put his hand over Bob's, he knew he'd lost any chance with Jessica. Damn, why had he done that?

It was always the same. The closeness he had with Bob led other people to the wrong conclusion. Normally neither of them cared and even made fun of the other cops who thought they were too friendly with each other.

Bob was to blame today, all because he thought they should be a gay couple to get into that club. "Forget it!" Steve realized belatedly he had spoken aloud.

"Forget what?" Bob searched his pocket for his car keys.

"Aw, forget it! Let's go question Enrico. I can stay in the car, since he knows my face." Steve felt resigned; this was a crapper of a day. Once he got off work, he was going to watch a cartoon marathon and fall asleep very late—or maybe not at all.

Was Enrico the one who had killed Randolph, all because he thought Steve was the new man in his lover's life? Steve shook himself, following Bob out of Dinah's. He realized he was watching Bob's butt and quickly looked away. Disturbing thoughts crossed his mind, of Bob lying next to him in bed, turning him on, and Steve shoved them away. He needed to get laid, and that couldn't happen soon enough.

"ENRICO MUST live in that apartment building over there." Bob stopped the car.

Surprised, Steve looked up at a Southwestern-style building with a red tiled roof. He'd been lost in thought during the entire drive. "Okay, you wanna do the questioning alone?"

Bob hesitated. "Don't know. Maybe he really shouldn't see you. I might get more information about you and your boyfriend Randolph," he teased.

Steve wasn't in the mood to counter. "Go ahead. I'll wait here," he said tersely.

Bob got out of the car. Steve watched him cross the road with long strides, seemingly determined to get the questioning behind him. Shifting in his seat, Steve craned his neck to see Bob enter the building. He had a bad feeling, letting his partner do the interrogation alone. What if Enrico got furious and attacked Bob?

Steve scolded himself for being overprotective, but on the other hand, they normally went in together. It was department protocol. To distract himself, he opened the glove compartment and found chocolate bar wrappers and old bills... and another paper with a written phone number. Did the number belong to a woman Bob had dated?

Steve stashed all the papers in his jeans pockets and looked outside to find a garbage can. Spotting one at the next corner, he was about to scramble out of the car when he saw that the backseat was littered with garbage as well. "Bob, you are a slob. Why do I put up with you?" Steve sighed and leaned over the seat backward to reach the trash scattered on the backseat. He had to wiggle around, and his red shirt pulled free of his jeans.

"Ewww!" he yelped. Something had brushed his back between his waistband and shirt. A spider? He jerked back, only to see Bob's grinning face through the open car window.

"Don't worry, buddy," Bob said. "I thought there was something on your back. It was nothing, though."

"Bob, I could kill you! You scared me to death!" Steve cried out, his heart racing.

"What's wrong, buddy?" Bob sounded concerned. "I was just teasing you."

"I'm phobic about spiders! As a kid I helped my parents to build a shed in our garden. Suddenly a big spider ran across the piece of wood I was carrying. Since then I can't stand spiders." Steve shuddered.

"If I had known…." Bob smiled apologetically.

"Forget it." Steve looked around and frowned. "Why are you back already? Did Enrico refuse to talk to you?"

"Worse. He's gone. I spoke with a neighbor, and he saw him leaving early today with a suitcase. Enrico seemed to be in a hurry. We should put an APB on him."

"Sure." While Bob got in and started the car, Steve grabbed the microphone and called Mary the dispatcher to send out an APB on Enrico Gonzales, suspect in the murder of Randolph Foreman.

"My God, if Enrico killed Randolph, I shouldn't have left them alone on Tuesday evening. Maybe I could have prevented Randolph's death." Steve felt miserable. He tried to remember the scene after Enrico opened the door and saw him and Randolph in a kind of embrace.

At least it must have looked like that to Gonzales. Enrico had been really angry when he'd accused Randolph of being with another man.

"Need your notebook, pal," Steve said.

Bob moved one arm to give Steve access to his inner jacket pocket. Steve opened the little book and gave a small whistle. "You got

Randolph's address. And he has a sister in east Culver City. When did you get this? Do we have an address for her too?"

"The precinct secretary, Millie Swanson, gave it to me. The sister's info is on the next page." Bob slowed the car. "Maybe we'll get lucky and talk to her today." He peered at a street sign. "This is the wrong direction. We have to go that way." Bob changed lanes to turn left at the next intersection.

"Palm Drive," Steve said, looking at Jane Foreman's address. "That's quite a distance. After we talk to her, we can head home." Steve slouched back in his seat and yawned. "The reports can wait until tomorrow." He stretched out his legs and got them tangled in the floor mat. Growling under his breath, he shoved the plastic mat back into place and brushed off his sneaker. "We're going to that party at Steps to Heaven in my car, okay? Your old Mercedes needs a general overhaul. Your mat has holes in it!"

"Hold your horses, Steve!" Bob pointed a finger at him with a smug expression. "Remember your passenger door? No lady would want to deal with that damn thing. Not to mention the greasy food you eat."

Steve kept silent. It was all Bob's fault. Bob had spoiled his chances of a date with Jessica with his ridiculous charade that they were gay. It was time to have some time alone, without his ever-present partner.

"THIS IS the right door. It says 'Jane Foreman' on the nameplate. Ring the bell." Steve shuffled from one foot to the other. He needed to go to the bathroom.

Bob pressed the button and got his badge out to show the woman.

"Who's there?" They heard a tiny voice, and the door opened a slit.

"Hello, ma'am. Detectives Curry and Randall from CCPD, may we speak with you?" Bob held up his ID.

"Of course. Is this about my brother?" Jane Foreman let them in. She was petite, with ash-blonde curls that reached to her shoulders. It was obvious she had been crying. She looked miserable.

"Miss Foreman, I hope we aren't disturbing you," Bob started.

Always a gentleman, huh? Steve thought. *You have a way with victims and women. They all melt when they hear your soft, compassionate voice.*

"We'd like to ask you about the friends Randolph had and if he had any enemies."

"Excuse me," Steve interrupted. "Can I use the bathroom, please?"

Bob met Steve's gaze, and Steve could hear what he was thinking. *"Why didn't you go at Dinah's? How often do I tell you not to wait so long?"*

Fuck you! Steve thought and sent a glare back at Bob.

"The door on the right," Jane Foreman whispered, pointing to the hall.

Steve smiled at her and hurried to relieve his bladder. When he came back, Bob was sitting on the edge of the couch, and Jane was leaning against the cushions beside him.

"So you said your brother had relations with other male models, but those didn't last long, and they all left him. You said Randolph and Enrico had an argument last Tuesday. Enrico didn't show up for the photo shoot, and Randolph felt bad," Bob summed up what Jane had told him.

Steve butted in, taking a seat in a chair opposite the other two. "Did Randolph talk to you about that club Steps to Heaven?"

Jane frowned. She pushed a strand of hair behind her ear and looked at Steve. "I remember him talking about a new place to meet interesting people. He said people at that club had real chances to break into showbiz, and he wanted to be a member too." She paused, looking pensive. "He also mentioned that some people he knew from the studio had joined the club and had stopped working for Fashion Photos. He sounded as if he knew something else but didn't want to talk with me about it."

Steve leaned forward. "It could be a great help if you remembered anything else. Maybe Randolph mentioned something more about what happened in that club?"

Jane smiled tiredly. "You know, Randolph was a bit dramatic. One day he loved people, the next day he felt rejected and wanted to

take revenge on them. But he was my brother, and I don't understand...."
Tears began to well up in her eyes.

Bob motioned Steve to stop the questioning. They had heard enough. "We're sorry for your loss, Miss Foreman." Bob placed a small card with their number on her coffee table. "If you think of anything else, give us a call. We'll see ourselves out."

Jane nodded, dabbing at her eyes.

When they left Jane Foreman's apartment, Steve said, "That's it, I've had enough for today. Will you take me home? I need some shut-eye. On Monday we can put our noses to the grindstone."

Bob glanced at him with a frown.

Steve knew Bob must think he was acting weirdly. There were very few weekends that they didn't see each other. There had always been time for a couple of beers or a dinner together before they went out on dates with their ladies. This weekend shouldn't be different, but Steve wasn't in the mood to spend his free time with Bob. The worst of it was that there was no lady in sight who could help him satisfy his needs.

Bob stopped the car in front of the small driveway that led to Steve's apartment. "What about a...?" Bob started.

Steve had to avert his eyes. He suddenly felt weak looking in Bob's eyes. He could not give in to this strange infatuation.

"I'm tired. See you on Monday, okay?" he said instead, and left the car without patting his partner or clasping hands as they usually did.

Chapter Five

STEVE ENTERED his apartment and inhaled deeply. Finally he was alone and had a long weekend ahead. The familiar scent of his place surrounded him, and nobody bothered him with teasing questions and useless reprimands. He trudged into the kitchen to get a beer, found an old slice of pizza in the fridge, and smiled in satisfaction.

Hey, Bob, who cares what I'm eating? Mm, this is so good.

After the second bite, Steve realized the pizza had a sour taste. Disgusted, he threw the food into the trash can. Looking in the cupboard for something else edible, he discovered some bottles with strange labels that he didn't recognize. They must be the ingredients for Bob's energy drinks. Why had Bob left them here?

Bob was over so often he'd become part of Steve's life. Steve had lost count of the days Bob crashed on his couch after a long night. In the morning Bob would jog to the nearby drug store and get stuff to make his special drinks.

Steve took a big gulp from the beer can, went to the living room, and plopped down on the sofa. His tight jeans were uncomfortable, and he decided to change into sweats. He got up again, leaving the beer on the coffee table. Unbuckling his jeans, he walked into the bedroom to finish undressing. Some crumbled papers slipped out of the jeans pocket, and he remembered the trash he had collected in Bob's car. He folded the jeans neatly and picked up the papers to store them temporarily on the bedside table.

Steve found light green sweats and pulled them on, but they hung so low on his hips he was afraid the pants would fall off. *Damn, Bob, they must be yours.* He groaned and rummaged in the closet for his own sweats.

Since there was nothing to do and very little to eat in the kitchen, Steve sprawled on the couch and sipped one of Bob's drinks. He had to admit it didn't taste that bad, a combination of pineapple and coconut.

Steve peered at the paper with the phone number from Bob's car, reluctant to throw it away. It didn't look familiar. Maybe one of Bob's dates?

Steve finished his drink. What if he dialed that number to find out who it was?

"Hello?" a female voice answered.

Steve was at a loss. He couldn't immediately match the voice to anyone he knew, but she sounded familiar. "Who's there? Maybe I dialed the wrong number," he said, feeling stupid for having phoned a stranger.

"Is it you, Steve Randall?"

All of a sudden, he recognized the Texan accent. "Luna? Lovely Luna?"

"Sure, it's me. Boy, is something wrong with you or Bob? You need any help?" Luna sounded compassionate and concerned.

Steve searched for what to say because he didn't want to admit he hadn't called her specifically.

"Huh, not at all, Luna. It's just… I could use some nice company, and wanted to ask if you have time to have dinner with me anytime soon." He inhaled deeply, waiting for her answer.

"Sure, why not. For you, anytime. Let me check my calendar, though…."

What was he supposed to say to her? Luna worked as a hooker. Once, they had rescued her from a lunatic who was about to kill her. Since then, they were friends. She had a soft spot for Bob, though, and whenever they met her, Steve wasn't even sure she noticed him at all.

"Okay, sweetie, what about Saturday night? Where's Bob? I can't imagine you without him. Will he come too?"

Steve bit his tongue and lied. "Naw, he's busy this weekend. I'll come around, let's say, about eight o'clock? You can choose the place to eat."

Luna answered with a soft "See you then, Steve."

The line went dead. Steve leaned back against the cushions with mixed feelings. While he was glad to have the weekend to himself, the thought of Bob sitting home alone, reading or drawing one of his portraits, left him uncomfortable. Bob had an amazing talent that allowed him to transfer emotions onto a face he drew. Once he had told Steve about an art competition at college where he had won the first prize with a portrait of his mother. Steve could watch Bob create his colored pencil drawings for hours.

Steve sighed, imagining Bob alone without any company.

What crap!

Most likely Bob was having dinner right now with some lovely lady. Possibly the lady who ran the vegetarian restaurant not far from his apartment. Bob had had a crush on her since she had opened the little restaurant a few months ago, and he certainly wouldn't give up a chance to go out with her. What was her name? Lucille, that was it. Her lasagna was one of Bob's favorite dishes. Lucille probably had several other specialties Bob would enjoy....

The real truth here was that he missed Bob more than he wanted to admit, and he was acting stupidly by pushing him away because he was upset about Randolph coming on to him—and ending up dead. Now Steve had gone to Luna, of all people, in a weak moment. Would Bob tease Steve if he found out? Or try to dig deep to discover what was bothering him? Confused, Steve kept picturing Bob's long slender fingers working with brush and paint.

He got up from the couch and hurried around cleaning up the house. He washed his favorite jeans. Bob often teased him because the jeans were so tight that they looked painted on.

Steve grinned in anticipation of the coming day. He would look great, and Lovely Luna would forget about her favorite cop—at least for a while.

IT WAS Saturday evening and Steve checked in the mirror one last time. His old corduroy jacket looked new again with the red silk tie and modish brown slacks. Satisfied, he stepped out his front door, making sure he had enough money and his keys.

Much to his regret, the full beauty of the newly polished Thunderbird didn't show up in the fading daylight. He'd used a new oil on the dashboard and backseat, and Lovely Luna would surely appreciate the aroma. Steve had seen the advertisement for the car treatment a while back and couldn't resist buying a product that claimed to "make your car sexy." Whistling, he started the car. He hadn't driven more than a mile when an odd smell filled his nose, and he cranked down the window. *Must have been a skunk near the car.*

Driving across Culver City to Luna's place, Steve realized he hadn't heard from Bob in the last forty-eight hours. Bob must be enjoying himself and didn't need Steve's company. Which was just as it should be.

"HI THERE." Steve embraced Luna and gave her a kiss on the cheek. "You look great, as always," he said, leading her to his car. He admired her tight black pants suit and long blonde hair.

"Your car always looks so tidy, completely the opposite of Bob's car." Luna smiled. Steve opened the door forcefully, and Luna got in. She frowned and sniffed. "By the way, I hope there wasn't a cat hiding in your car. It smells as if…." She hesitated, looking at Steve.

"Can't be, don't know any cats," Steve assured her. "During their inspection the guys at the garage must have put an air freshener in the car." *Another lie*, he thought. "Where to?" he sidetracked, cursing his idea to buy that oil for his car.

Luna pointed at the next block. "If you don't mind, we can walk there. It's a little bistro, and they serve delicious antipasti."

"Okay, it's a nice evening, and a walk would do me good. Come on, then." He got out of the car, helped her out, and took her arm. They walked down the street and around the block to Auntie's Pasta. Some people were sitting outside on a small patio, enjoying their spaghetti and linguini.

Luna shivered and shook her head, "Too chilly out here." They went inside, and the host seated them at a nice table by a window.

While Luna studied the menu, Steve looked at her. She was strikingly beautiful, with fine features. She could have been a fashion model instead of a prostitute if her fortunes had been better. Luna had become a really good friend to him and Bob. Her job as a working girl had caused her trouble more than once, and Steve and Bob had helped her get rid of demanding customers. On the other hand, she had provided information that had helped solve cases.

"Dear, have you chosen already? A penny for your thoughts," Luna said with concern.

"I'll have what you have." Steve put the menu aside and looked around.

"The men's room is over there," Luna said.

Steve stared at her. For one moment he was sure he'd heard Bob speak. Steve flushed, surprised how much he suddenly missed Bob. They should have taken Luna out together, to repay her for the many things she'd done for them. *And he'd lied to her, saying Bob was too busy.*

"Thanks. Be right back." In the restroom Steve splashed cold water on his face with his cupped hands. Being there with Luna gave him a case of the guilts. Luna must be wondering why only one of her two favorite cops was sitting with her in a restaurant for dinner, but she seemed too polite to ask Steve directly.

Deep inside, Steve knew the answer: he was trying to prove his masculinity by dating a beautiful woman.

Dinner together wouldn't do any harm, he told himself. Luna was always nice to chat with. Her stories about the strange situations she'd been in with clients were good for a laugh or a groan. He just wished Bob was there with them to enjoy the meal and lively conversation. Steve had never spent time with Luna without him, and he felt lonely.

When he came back to their table, Luna had ordered already. She raised a glass of red wine, waiting until Steve had his in his hand.

"To my favorite cops," she said, her eyes sparkling in the light from the candle on the table.

"To you." Steve clinked his glass with hers. He tasted the wine with enjoyment. He wasn't an experienced wine drinker like Bob, but he savored the smooth grape flavor and heady aroma.

A young waitress came over with two plates, putting one in front of each of them. "Bon appétit!" she called out.

"I hope you like crab cakes," Luna said, handing over his knife and fork.

"How did you know?" Steve smiled. He didn't waste any time and took a bite. Bob had first introduced him to the spicy little cakes a couple of years earlier. Bob had ordered crab cakes at a little place in Santa Rosa, and as usual, Steve had sampled off his plate. Delicious! Steve had loved crab cakes ever since. Damn, even the meal reminded him of Bob!

They ate, content to sit together without needing to talk. Steve felt relaxed, Lovely Luna's familiar company lifting his mood.

"Some more wine?" the young waitress asked after a while, taking the empty bottle.

Steve nodded. "Yes, please. What about a dessert, Luna? I'd like an ice cream with cherries and whipped cream."

"No, thanks," she laughed. "I'm full. But take whatever you want. It's amazing what you can eat without gaining weight."

Steve felt her gaze on his body, and it made him warm inside, a sensation he hadn't had for a long time. He tried to convince himself that it was a reaction to the wine. On the other hand, why shouldn't he feel excited after a compliment from a beautiful woman?

They drank the rest of their wine until the ice cream arrived. Steve licked his spoon, making a show of enjoying the sweet dessert. He managed to coax Luna into taking a bite of ice cream. Steve found himself watching her every move as she licked the spoon, her pink tongue darting out to get every bit.

"It's really delicious, Steve." Luna smacked her lips one last time. "What a nice Saturday evening! It's always interesting to talk with you. But something's worrying you." She placed her hand on top of his. "If it's okay with you, we can have some coffee at my apartment before you go home." She wiggled her eyebrows and made Steve laugh. "I know Bob will be lonely this weekend without you." Luna patted his hand, a complete professional. She would understand if he cut things short. "So if you have to go straight home?"

Steve shook his head. "No problem, Luna. Let's go and have that coffee. Just the right thing after dinner." He waved at the busy girl serving the other patrons. "The check, please!"

TEN MINUTES later Steve sat sprawled on Lovely Luna's couch, balancing a steaming mug of sweet coffee. Luna had taken off her black suit jacket and settled comfortably in the corner, leaning against the cushions.

"You've been busy solving one case after the other these last few weeks." She leaned forward to snag a box of cigarettes from the table.

"Yeah, the last one was unnerving for me," Steve mused, grabbing the lighter from the table to light her cigarette.

"Thanks." She inhaled deeply and looked at Steve. "What happened, sweetheart?"

Steve hesitated for a moment, not wanting to delve into memories of his time with Randolph and the whole subsequent murder investigation.

A silky, sock-clad foot nudged Steve's thigh. "Spill it, there's nothing I haven't heard before," Luna said softly, resting her foot against Steve's leg.

"It started with Bob's friend Linda, who is a model. We went to watch her photo shoot. The photographer, Randolph, wanted me to model swimsuits for a magazine shoot," Steve started, watching Luna for any negative reaction. To his surprise, Luna didn't say a word, looking at him intently. Encouraged, he told her everything: about Bob and Linda convincing him to model for Randolph, then Randolph pressing Steve to kiss him, and Randolph's death the following day.

"You know, Bob is such a pain in the ass lately." Steve knew he sounded hurt and childish, but he couldn't help it. "He promised to pick me up at the photo studio but was late because he stayed too long with Linda and got stuck in a traffic jam." He took a deep breath.

Luna frowned. "What happened? You seem angry with Bob." She wrapped her hands around her mug and took a sip of coffee.

"What really ticked me off was that I was trying to make a play for a girl named Jessica," Steve went on. "We need to go undercover to a nightclub, and Bob made it seem like he and I were a couple, so the chick backed off. She's going to get us into the club called Steps to Heaven." Steve realized he was holding Luna's ankle while talking. Self-consciously, he put his hand in his lap.

"Hey, keep your hand there. It felt fine," she purred. "Tell me about that partner of yours. In my opinion, Bob has always had eyes for you. Does that make you uncomfortable?" Luna stubbed out her cigarette and slid her legs into Steve's lap. She wiggled her toes.

Steve took a deep breath. "I don't know what's wrong lately. I've never felt uncomfortable when people teased me and Bob about being too close. It's the way we are. But when Randolph came on to me, it felt really strange." Steve smiled shyly.

"I can understand." Luna stopped wiggling her toes and looked expectantly at him.

He cleared his throat. "For that, Bob wants to go undercover as a gay couple. That makes me very uncomfortable." Steve kept his disturbing and confusing thoughts about Bob to himself.

"You and Bob will work it out, I'm sure." Luna nudged his hand with her foot. "What about a massage?"

"My pleasure." Steve began rubbing the balls of her feet. She groaned, letting out a satisfied breath. "Oh, you like that?" He grinned, stroking her delicate feet.

"Nothin' better, darlin'," Luna sighed. She relaxed against the corner of the couch, her eyes closed.

Steve ran his thumb up the arch of her foot. His thoughts went to their upcoming undercover assignment at Steps to Heaven.

"Luna?"

"Mmm, spill it," she said lazily, lighting a new cigarette.

"What do you know about Steps to Heaven?"

Luna shook her head, twirling her hair around one finger. "It's just a drug den. I don't know why you want to go to that club. Hopefuls wanting a career go there to talk to movie producers and directors, but all they get is drugs and lost dreams. I know a couple of girls who started out right, in modeling, but are now on the streets."

"What have you heard about Blue Rocket?" Steve asked, admiring the way her broad black belt made her waist look so small and how her silky blouse molded to her breasts.

"That's nasty stuff. I've used marijuana on occasion." She grinned mischievously, the smoke from the cigarette swirling lazily above her head. "You won't tell the cops, will you?"

"Scout's honor," he promised. "Drug-related deaths have increased in Culver City since Blue Rocket was introduced on the street, and we're concerned they might be due to the opening of that club."

"My friend Marcy was a member for a short time. She said her heart was practically jumping out of her chest when she snorted Blue Rocket. She stopped taking it, afraid of the side effects."

"We think someone is experimenting with the new stuff and doesn't care about the consequences," Steve said grimly. "Any idea who the owner of the club is?"

"I'm afraid I can't help you," Luna said. Then she snapped her fingers. "Marcy mentioned a doctor, very famous and well-known in the modeling business. But don't ask me who it is."

Steve continued the massage of her feet. "We'll find those responsible!" he said grimly.

"I'm sure, darlin'." Luna moved her feet to one side and purred happily when he massaged her heels.

Steve felt better too. It had helped to let Luna in on their case. Leaning back against the couch, he continued to rub Luna's feet. He had wanted to talk about Bob, about the way their partnership almost felt like a burden and his own confusion and personal needs. Instead the warmth of Luna's feet felt so good against his palms, and to his surprise, his jeans got tighter—he was aroused.

"Ugh," he croaked and tried to sit up to... to put some distance between him and Luna's feet resting on his crotch.

Luna put her feet on the floor. "This is nice, but I'm not sure I'm actually who you want," she said astutely. "I wouldn't say no either." She stubbed her cigarette in the ashtray and went to the kitchen.

Steve watched her walk, feeling his groin swell. Her tight pants outlined her long legs and ass nicely.

"Here's what my mom always gave me whenever I was in a bad mood or felt unhappy. I still bake them from time to time." Smiling, she offered him a box of small sugar cookies with chocolate in the middle.

"They look delicious!" He took one and was about to put it in his mouth when Luna stopped him with one hand on his.

"Wait a sec. These are chocolate kisses." Luna smiled and retrieved the cookie, pressing the sugary morsel against his lips. "Here you are." She fed Steve the cookie.

"Mmm, really good," he murmured, the cookie and the candy melting together in his mouth with a burst of sweetness.

"If you need a kiss as well, I will happily oblige. What are friends for?" She bent down, bracing herself lightly against his shoulders.

Steve closed his eyes expectantly.

"Oops!" she cried out and landed in Steve's lap.

He encircled her warm body with his arms and looked into her laughing eyes.

"Lost my balance." She giggled.

"No problem at all, Luna." Steve nuzzled her neck. Her long hair was everywhere, in his face and tickling his chest through the half-open shirt. She wiggled to get up again, but Steve held her tight, inhaling her sweet scent.

"That kiss...?" he murmured against her hair, and she stopped moving away from him.

"Dear friend, I hope I can make you feel better," she said softly, and then her lips were on his.

The long pent-up hunger for a woman was overwhelming. Tasting Luna, savoring her kiss, was like a balm on his soul. Because she was a woman he knew very well and who had always been supportive, it was easier to lose himself in the tender kiss they shared. Just one kiss wasn't enough for him, and his tongue had its own ideas. Luna didn't withdraw when he claimed her mouth fiercely.

With a soft moan, she let him in and responded to his eager tongue.

They drew back to catch their breath. Steve averted his eyes. "I'm sorry, Luna, don't know why—"

"Shh," she soothed him, cupping his face with her hands. "You needed it, and you know I love you dearly. Let's go over there. It's more comfortable. We can spend the night together. I could use a friend like you tonight, as well." She smiled, getting off his lap. Taking his hand, she pulled him up and led him toward the bedroom.

Feeling like he was in a trance, Steve followed her, the taste of her still on his mouth. His jeans were even tighter at the groin, and he couldn't shove aside thoughts of what lay ahead. He and Luna—together!

The next moment Luna's hands were on him, helping him out of his shirt.

"Yeah, Luna...." He didn't resist when she unbuckled his jeans and pulled them down. He was surprised that he felt embarrassed standing in front of her in his briefs. *Is this really a good idea? What will Bob think if he finds out?*

"Let me take care of you, darling," Luna said seductively. She walked to the bed and opened the duvet. "Slip in. I'll be back in a minute." She turned and went to the bathroom.

Steve snuggled into the sheets and tried to gather his thoughts. What was he doing here? What had made him call Luna, have dinner with her, and go back to her apartment?

And now he was lying in her bed, like a.... Steve paused, unwilling to compare himself to one of her customers. No, Luna was his friend, a friend he had always respected and envied for her fondness of Bob. If Bob knew....

"I see you're getting comfortable, that's good. I'm a bit chilled. Can you warm me?" Luna had put on dark blue silky pajamas. She did a slow turn as if showing off the outfit before climbing into bed and pulling the covers over them. She hugged him, snuggling him close. "Don't get me wrong, dear. I don't want to make you feel guilty." Luna placed a chaste kiss on his cheek. "Let's enjoy each other's company, and maybe you'll feel like telling me some stories of your life."

Steve felt her smile against his neck and wondered why he felt so good with her. He shifted toward her and realized that his erection had almost gone. *Probably better that way,* he thought, regretting it at the same time. He sighed and put his arms around Luna.

"It's good to be with you," he murmured, inhaling her scent. *Something like roses.* He nipped on her earlobe and traced the inside, making her giggle.

"Steve, that's my ticklish spot. Don't you dare!"

She giggled, and he felt her soft breasts, through the fabric of her pajamas, on his hand. Without thinking he let his hand linger, feeling a nipple harden. Luna accepted his hand, arching up against him. Steve teased the nub, drawing back when Luna moaned lightly.

"Do that again," she whispered, snuggling even closer.

Steve put an arm around her waist, lifting her pajama top to feel naked skin under his palms.

Luna shuddered. "Man, your hands are cold. Gimme those." She briskly rubbed his hands between hers, restoring blood flow.

He smiled, continuing his journey under the edge of her silky top. Luna gasped when Steve found the other nipple and circled it with two fingers, making it harden. Their lips met for another kiss, and Steve felt his cock twitch and respond to the warmth of the woman by his side.

"You like me," Luna said softly. She leaned on one elbow and looked down at him. "You are beautiful, and I envy anyone who gets the chance to live with you." She traced the outline of his jaw with one finger and caressed his cheek.

"I feel like nobody wants me. It's the job. I'm getting too old for this shit," Steve said, only half joking. The memory of lying in his bed, trying to arouse himself with fantasies of a woman, only to have thoughts of Bob intrude, flashed through his brain. "Luna, I must be nuts. Lately I worry I won't be able to get it up when I'm with a woman. And Bob makes it worse somehow."

"Stop talking about Bob right now," Luna said, running her hand over Steve's furry chest, lingering here and there. Smiling, she drew the covers back, placing her hands on his cotton-covered crotch.

"Hey," he said weakly, not trusting his body. "You see, it'll be useless." He shifted, but she held on, not ready to release him yet.

"What're you talking about, Steve? I see a strong and healthy man." She stroked his cock through the fabric of his briefs. "You're all tense. You should tell me. Get it off your chest, and you'll feel better."

Luna trailed her hand lightly over him and sat back against the head of the bed. Steve did the same. Cross-legged, they looked at each other, the sexual atmosphere draining away.

Steve cleared his throat. "I can't stand Bob anymore. He's everywhere in my life, and I can't remember a day that I didn't spend time with him."

Luna gave a little sigh, reminding Steve of her deep affection for Bob.

"Because of his constant presence, I have no personal life. He criticizes me, makes fun of me, and he's a know-it-all."

Luna nodded. Her eyes were full of understanding. Steve took a deep breath. Just talking about his problems made him feel better.

"Well, Steve, what do you want from me? Call Bob, so you can give him a talking-to?" When he didn't answer, she grabbed the phone from the side table.

"Don't," Steve said softly. "I'm a dumbass. I want you to hold me, and I apologize for rambling. I was lonely this weekend and needed to be with someone familiar." *Oh my God, I sound like Randolph.*

"It's a deal. But no further complaints about other lovers," Luna said with a grin. She snuggled against him, kissing him the way a sister would.

More relaxed than he had been in weeks, he curled against her and fell asleep.

STEVE AWOKE with the urgent need to relieve his bladder. It was still dark. His wristwatch showed 4:30 a.m., the early hours of Sunday morning. A glance to the right told him Luna was sound asleep.

He didn't dare switch on a light and carefully made his way through the shadowy room to the bathroom. When he returned he looked at the covers around Luna's hips and the way her pajama top had slipped off to reveal a naked shoulder. He slid into bed, stretching out, savoring the warmth her body offered.

Luna moved in her sleep and snuggled up to him, her knee resting on his thigh. She put one arm on his belly and rubbed small circles around his belly button. Steve felt his cock react, and before he could turn away, she had cupped his briefs again. This time she didn't waste any time. She slid her fingers beneath the underwear and stroked the hardening flesh.

"Are you awake?" Steve asked huskily.

"No. What about you?" she answered languidly.

"I'm still dreaming," Steve whispered.

Lying back, he let Luna do her magic with his excited cock. Her fingers tightened around his balls, squeezing gently. Luna sucked her finger to moisten it, then slipped it between his legs and teased his opening, circling the sensitive rim with her slick fingertip. He arched upward to give her better access. Luna was experienced, and she kept up an erotic seesaw of sensations between stroking his cock and manipulating her finger in his opening. Steve gasped, overwhelmed, and he came with a deep moan, covering her hand with his semen.

When he had enough breath, he whispered, "Thanks."

Luna touched his face gently, wiping off the sweat, before kissing his cheek.

"This is between us, okay?" Steve asked.

Luna nodded, wearing a look of immense wisdom. This was what she did every day, but still, to Steve it was special and had helped him tremendously. Relieved, he pushed her hair off her lovely face. He still felt like he was dreaming, even when he took her in his arms once more. He had slept with a woman, and she had shown him that he was a healthy man.

Chapter Six

MONDAY MORNING. Bob had eyes, and he could see that Steve was running hot and cold, but he had no clue what was causing this puzzling behavior. After Steve's decidedly abrupt and unfriendly parting on Thursday, Bob expected a grumpy partner on Monday morning. Instead, Steve bounced into the squad room with a cheerful, "What's up, folks?"

"Let's catch the bad guys and clean the streets of Culver City!" he exclaimed, rolling up his sleeves. He took a folder from his desk and frowned. "Bob, where's the APB on Enrico Gonzales? It's time to get that weasel arrested and questioned." With an intense expression, Steve flipped hurriedly through the folder.

"It's where you left it on Thursday, remember?" Bob pointed out calmly, pushing some other papers aside. "Here you are."

"Always looking on the bright side of life, right?" Steve said.

Bob paused. Steve's smile had a false, forced quality, as if he was trying way too hard to be cheerful. *What was going on?* "No, hardly ever," Bob said quietly. "Especially after having to cope with a partner who doesn't show up in the morning to pick me up." He couldn't resist adding, "If you decide to have an all-night party, you could at least inform me that I have to get to the station alone."

"Wha—? How do you...?" Steve sounded like he'd swallowed a rock.

Bob saw a light blush creep over Steve's face. He nodded without much satisfaction. "So I'm right. I only hope she was worth it." Bob got up and strode to the door, leaving behind an openmouthed Steve.

Anger boiling in his throat, Bob hurried to the men's room. He was such a fool, lashing out at Steve because he'd had to wait for a ride that never showed. Steve was often late. Rollins usually got in a lather about latecomers, threatening all sorts of punishments that he never meted out. Steve was lucky that he only had to cope with Bob's annoyance for once.

Bob used the urinal and washed his hands, checking himself in the mirror. He looked tired after an almost sleepless night. The weekend had been a bust. He'd kept busy with the laundry on Friday. What had he done on Saturday? Slept in, although he normally got up early to jog through the park. All weekend something had been missing… Steve's presence. Bob had sorely missed Steve's babbling about whatever weird news he had read, his complaints that Bob had nothing edible at his place, and his goofy exuberance. Steve could always cheer him up. Bob knew Steve would have a reason for spending the weekend without him. There had been no parting pat on the shoulder Thursday evening, leaving Bob confused and insecure.

He was used to having Steve around, even on their days off. Bob had to find a life of his own. Steve was trying to move on, and Bob had to do the same. Steve had probably spent his time with a woman, while Bob had been sitting around feeling useless and lonely. With a sense of purpose, Bob resolved to work out more regularly and lose some weight. He was pinching his waist, checking for extra pounds, when the door opened.

"Chris Barber is waiting in interrogation room five. Would you mind doing your job, or do you need some assistance here?" an impatient Steve called from the hallway.

Steve's sparkling eyes told Bob they were back to their old banter.

"I've been waiting for you!" Bob said, brushing his hair back. "Again—but you were late. Next time I'll ask Officer Simon." Bob knew Steve didn't like the nosy officer at all.

Wordlessly, Steve grabbed him by the arm and propelled him out the door. "Don't you dare. You're stuck with me. Capeesh?" Bob felt

Steve's breath tingle against his neck. He tried to ignore it, but had to admit he liked the sensation.

Back to business. Bob let Steve drag him down to the interrogation room. Steve had to stay in a side room, observing the questioning behind two-way mirrors. Bob saw him, his arms tightly crossed over his chest, but otherwise, he didn't appear offended that he had to stay away from Barber.

Bob walked into the main interrogation room, motioning an officer out. Chris Barber regarded Bob with a quizzical expression. He obviously didn't understand why he was there and was impatient about having to wait so long.

"Mr. Barber, we need to know what happened last Tuesday, September 3." Bob sat down opposite Chris Barber, leafing through the folder in front of him.

"What happened? Nothing! When I left the studio, that new guy with the dark hair—your friend?—was still there. I had a meeting with my boss, Mr. Sanders." Chris wrung his hands, nervous and tense. "Randolph was supposed to meet us, but he never showed."

"What time was the meeting with Mr. Sanders, and how long did you wait for Randolph?" Bob asked, making sure that the interrogation was being taped.

"We met at eight thirty at Charly's, and I left the restaurant about 10:30 p.m. and went home," Chris said. "I always sleep late. My landlady, Mrs. Stuart, rang the bell late in the morning, about eleven, to remind me that the cleaners were coming to wash the carpet on the stairs."

"Randolph was found dead the next afternoon, on Wednesday. Any idea who could have killed him?" Bob stared at Chris Barber. He saw the nervousness in the young man's face and decided to push him further. "Did you have any problems with Randolph?"

"What? Me?" Chris's face went red.

"Why not?" Bob shrugged. "You wouldn't be the first one who fell in love with a man and got out of control. Were you jealous?"

"You must be kidding. You should ask Enrico Gonzales, Randy's latest lover. They had arguments, and more than once Enrico was late for the shoot. I think it was the same last Tuesday. Maybe he was the one who—" Chris stopped talking.

"We'll take care of that." Bob bent forward in his seat. "One more question. What was your meeting with Sanders and Randolph about?"

Chris relaxed visibly. "We needed Randolph's good connections to the East Coast. Sanders was expecting a big deal with Glamour, one of the most famous photo studios in New York. We wanted Randy to prepare the deal."

"Okay." Bob nodded, stopping the recording.

"Can I go?" Barber squirmed on his seat.

"In case you intend to leave town, please inform the police," Bob got up and walked around the table.

"Do I need to get a lawyer?" Barber bristled. "I wasn't planning on going anywhere. Except out of here! I do have a job, with clients and models who need to be photographed. You people have already disrupted business at the studio quite enough."

"You can go now." Bob pointed to the door.

Chris Barber left the room.

Bob did a few quick neck exercises to relieve his tight shoulders and collected the papers on the table. He left the interrogation room and walked down the stairs to the second floor. He was about to swing the squad room door open, when it was pushed from the inside, and Steve almost ran into him.

"Whoa, buddy, hold your horses!" Bob stumbled back, overbalanced, and grabbed hold of Steve's arm.

"We gotta run. Enrico is ours!" Steve said excitedly. "I just got notice, he was busted in a cheap motel in Bakersfield. And he wasn't alone."

"Who was he with?" Bob asked, taking a quick moment to toss the notes from Barber's interrogation onto his desk before running to catch up with his partner.

"The arresting officers didn't say." Steve hopped lightly on the balls of his feet, impatient to get going. "I can't wait to talk turkey with him. I can still see his eyes when he came into Randolph's office and saw the two of us—Randolph was trying to kiss me! If looks could kill." Steve shuddered, obviously remembering the last time he had seen Randolph alive.

"Why'd Enrico go all the way to Bakersfield?"

"Dunno." Steve dragged Bob farther along the hall to the parking garage. "We're gonna meet him at the police headquarters in Bakersfield. I talked to the chief there, and he agreed to let us talk to the suspect since the crime was committed in Culver City. Come on, let's not waste any time."

That's so Steve, always on the move. "We should inform Rollins. He...."

"Rollins called in sick." Steve waved away his objections.

"Then we inform Lieutenant Copperfield," Bob insisted and left for the squad room.

"You're right, as always," Steve admitted. When Bob came back, he offered, "We can take my car, it's polished and waxed, but don't mention the nasty smell." Steve made a face.

"Huh?"

"I used that spray I bought some time ago, but obviously it isn't to everybody's taste. You'll see." Steve pushed the down button of the elevator, shuffling from one foot onto the other.

Bob put his arm around his partner's shoulder to calm him down. "You really want to drive to Bakersfield to question Mr. Gonzales?" he asked. "We've got a lot to do here. We have the Brunner case, the last drug victims, and I'd like to check the reports on the drug-related deaths from the last few months." Bob stopped, patting Steve on the chest. "But I see we have to pursue Enrico—he's our main suspect."

Steve nodded. "I want to question him as soon as possible." Then Steve smiled sheepishly. "Maybe we can drop briefly into Christy's on the way out to Bakersfield. I got this new Yamamoto watch, and there's a couple of functions that I just can't figure out."

"Steve, what are we talking about here? You need to do some errands?" Bob shook his head, feeling his patience beginning to drain away. "Do it on your own free time. What did you do last weekend? You had plenty of time to get your watch fixed."

"I got kinda busy with other stuff," Steve said with a dreamy smile.

Seeing Steve's moony expression, Bob knew there was a woman involved. Apparently Steve had pretended he wanted to be alone on the weekend because he'd had a hookup. Bob's mood sank.

The fact that his partner needed to get laid had been obvious since their last talk at Dinah's diner, when Jessica thought they were a couple. Bob groaned, feeling a tingling in his groin. *What about my own needs? I could have had the chance to date Linda. She's given me enough hints that she wouldn't object to a night with me.* He had refused because he'd promised to pick up Steve at the photo studio. And, honestly, he wasn't interested in her. She was gorgeous and fun but just not what he was looking for.

Something was definitely wrong with him.

"Up or down?" Officer Simon stood in the open door of the elevator, glaring at the two daydreaming cops.

"Down." Steve stepped in the elevator, rubbing his wrist with the new watch. Bob followed, nodding at the officer.

"Any news in the dead photographer's case? There are rumors—" Simon started.

"What rumors, Simon? Don't you have a case file waiting on your desk? Go run down some snitches or something to fill your day," Steve said snidely.

"Rumors are flying all over, Steve." Simon winked crudely at him. "Never know which ones to believe."

"Must be our floor!" Steve winked right back at him when the elevator door opened. "Yours is ladies' lingerie, isn't it?" He and Bob got off on the parking garage level.

"He's an idiot," Bob said, laughing at Steve's teasing. "You really want to take a two-hour drive to Bakersfield?"

"Bob, I can't wait to talk to Enrico," Steve said, pulling his keys out of his jeans pocket. "On the other hand, you mentioned in your report that Sanders said something about a Dr. Glassman. He had an appointment with him the day Randolph was shot. Dr. Glassman lives in Santa Barbara. We can pay him a visit and check out how long it takes to get there."

"Sanders said he got stuck in heavy traffic," Bob recalled. "Maybe we can find out if there was a traffic snarl, some kind of accident or roadwork on the 405." Bob was more intrigued with driving up to Bakersfield. At least he and Steve were working together smoothly. The earlier they solved the case, the better Steve would feel, and they would be back to their good old times. "It would be useful to take an overnight bag, in case we find out something there that needs following up," Bob thought out loud.

Steve nudged his side. "Now we are on the same page, partner. It won't take a lot of time to pack some things." Steve rushed across the parking garage to the Thunderbird. Even in the dim light, the car looked shiny and new.

"It must be love," Bob joked, moving his hand over the clean hood. Steve responded with a proud smile and unlocked his door. As usual Bob struggled to open the passenger door. "Damn!" he cursed and finally yanked it open. He slid into the seat and arranged his legs, exhaling deeply.

Steve drove out of the garage and accelerated. It was high noon. At this time of the day, the traffic wasn't too heavy, and Steve made good time.

"What's this?" Bob wrinkled his nose. "It smells as if a cat has—"

"I told you. It's the oil I bought." Steve shrugged, winding the side window down. A breeze of warm air, filled with exhaust fumes, entered the car and mingled with the lingering smell of the oil.

Bob leaned back against the headrest and closed his eyes. "I'm thinking about our suspects. What's Sanders's motive? Why would he want to murder Randolph, one of his best photographers? They wanted to expand the business to the East Coast and needed Randolph's connections. In Sanders's shoes, it would be stupid to eliminate a man he needed."

"After we've interrogated Enrico, we'll know more." Steve leaned an elbow on the open car window. The wind ruffled his hair. "Many people murder out of jealousy." He waggled a finger in Bob's direction. "It was a crime of passion, I'll bet you."

Changing the subject, he went on, "By the way, I gotta tell you that I didn't like the way you acted when I was trying to finesse Jessica the other—"

"Just because I want to go undercover as a couple? Steve, get over it. We've got too many cases on our plate." Bob frowned. "The party at the club could take us a step closer to the guys who are pushing Blue Rocket and other bad drugs." Relaxing a bit, he said, "Let's talk to the people, get an impression of what's going on there. Maybe we'll know more after the party." When he opened his eyes again, he looked around, confused. "Hey, I thought we were going to stop at my place first."

"Buddy, you have enough of your stuff at my place. Not to mention all your various energy drinks."

"Really? I hope you didn't drink them all." Bob raised an eyebrow.

Steve made a face, pulling the car to a halt in his driveway. "You wanna come up with me or wait in my precious car?"

"You'll do just fine packing our bag. I'm waiting here," Bob said, putting his sunglasses on.

"I'll be back in a minute." Steve got out of the car and swaggered to his apartment.

Bob smiled, glad that Steve's good mood was back. After a long weekend without him, Bob was looking forward to spending time with Steve, working and hopefully solving both their main cases. Bob knew the hard way what drugs could do to a person. Sue, a girl from his neighborhood, had been addicted to heroin and died at the age of seventeen. Ever since, Bob had been extra sensitive when drugs were involved. They had to find those responsible for the drug-related deaths. All the victims had been actors, actresses, and wannabe celebrities. Randolph had been their first solid link to a questionable business, and now he was dead. Could all the drug deaths be linked? Maybe this wasn't a straightforward case of jealousy, but a conspiracy to silence Randolph before he revealed what he knew about the club.

"Are you dreaming?" Steve asked through the car window.

Bob startled, realizing he had dozed off.

Steve looked at him with sparkling eyes and threw a small traveling bag onto the backseat. "Was it a hard night for you too?" He waggled one eyebrow.

"Yeah, didn't get a wink of sleep." Bob smiled, sitting up. "Okay, first up north to Santa Barbara. What's the address of that doctor?"

Steve shifted in his seat and fumbled in his jeans pocket, pulling out a crumpled paper. "Here's the address. 233 San Ysidro Road."

Bob fed the GPS with the address. "Ready to go! Now let's hurry!"

Steve started the car. Following the highway north, they listened to John Denver songs on the radio. It was early afternoon when they arrived in Montecito, a wealthy part of Santa Barbara. Dr. Glassman's practice was in a white office building.

Steve gave a whistle, reading the silver plaque next to the door.

"Bob, this doc does plastic surgery—just in case you want to have your face, or other parts of your body, lifted." Playfully Steve pinched Bob's waist.

Bob chuckled. "Stop taking advantage of my ticklish spot. I won't need a plastic surgeon for at least thirty years." He snorted, unconsciously putting his hand on his stomach. He didn't feel good in his own skin, which could be the reason he had refused Linda's offer.

Steve walked into the building slightly ahead of Bob and approached a huge reception desk, where a blonde woman was painting her nails. "Hello, we'd like to talk to Dr. Ruben Glassman." Steve beamed at her.

She ignored him, blowing on the nails to dry the pink polish.

"We're detectives from the Culver City Police Department." Bob pulled out his badge and pushed it under her nose. "And who are you?"

"I'm Debbie Schellenberg, Dr. Glassman's assistant." She put another layer of pink nail polish on her nails.

"Would you tell Dr. Glassman, or shall we just go in? We have to talk to him right away," Bob said sharply.

Steve glanced at him, mouthing, "You're a good bad cop."

The blonde heaved a sigh and gave a little pout of disapproval. She grabbed the phone receiver carefully to avoid damaging her freshly painted nails. "Doctor, two police officers are here to talk to you." She paused, frowning. "No, they don't have an appointment. What should I do with them?" Holding one hand out in front of her, she silently admired her nails, listening. "Okay, in a minute."

"We have a question. Can you show me your appointment schedule from last Tuesday and Wednesday?" Steve asked.

"Sure, why not?" Debbie sounded bored. She opened the upper drawer of her desk and took out a big book. She leafed through the pages. "Here are the appointments. What do you want to know?"

"If John Sanders was here last week and at what time he arrived." Bob took the book from her and checked the names.

"Let me see." Steve looked over Bob's shoulder and whistled after a moment. "Look here. Sanders arrived at 2:00 p.m. on Wednesday. Thanks so much, Debbie!" Steve beamed at her.

Bob handed the book back to Debbie. He was annoyed. Whenever Steve saw a woman, he went into flirting mode, and lately this behavior annoyed Bob in a way he couldn't understand. Glassman's assistant was nothing extraordinary, but Steve acted as if he had the woman of his dreams in front of him.

For the first time, the receptionist looked at the detectives. "Would you follow me? Dr. Glassman is waiting in his office." She got up, tottering on spike heels. "You'll have to be brief. He has another appointment at five o'clock."

She knocked on a wide wooden door and opened it for them. "Please, enter. Dr. Glassman?"

A tall man in his forties rose from behind his desk. He motioned the detectives to come inside and pointed to two broad armchairs in front of his desk. "What can I do for you?" Dr. Glassman gave his receptionist a smile. "Thank you, Deb."

Bob looked around, taking in the paintings on the wall of the big room. The polished furniture and decoration showed how prosperous the practice was. Dr. Ruben Glassman was a good-looking man, without a wrinkle on his movie-star-handsome face. His dark hair was carefully cut. Bob suspected that the doctor had gone under the knife himself to improve his looks. He wore an expensive tailored suit, which fostered his imposing façade.

Bob cleared his throat. "Detectives Steve Randall and Bob Curry, Culver City PD. We are investigating a murder in Culver City. John Sanders says he had an appointment with you last Wednesday, September 4."

Ruben Glassman pinched his nose. "Last Wednesday, you say? I was working in my practice, and John Sanders was visiting me. He's a friend of mine. John has consulted me many times. We help the starlets to look better, to be more competitive." Glassman looked at them questioningly.

Steve asked, "Do you know Randolph Foreman, a photographer?"

"Foreman? Randolph?" Dr. Glassman smiled. "Yes, I know Randy. He's a good photographer, with good connections to the East Coast. Sanders talked to me about expanding his business to the east, and Randy's going to be an important part in it. Why do you ask?" Glassman ran his hand along the shiny surface of his desk as if he wanted to wipe some specks of dust away.

"He was shot dead," Bob said curtly.

Glassman looked aghast. "No! That can't be true." He covered his mouth and bent forward in his armchair, obviously shocked by the bad news. "I remember Randolph being such a smart guy." He shook his head, looking perturbed. "That's awful. Detectives, I'm so sorry. How can I help you?"

"We have to check the movements of all persons who were connected with Randolph Foreman. You said you were here last Wednesday. What about Tuesday?" Bob opened his notepad and looked for his pen.

"Sirs, you can't ask me that seriously. I'm a busy man, sometimes here, sometimes there." Glassman looked contrite.

"We want to see your appointment book." Steve handed Bob his pen, turning toward Glassman. "Tell us about the night from Tuesday to Wednesday, Doctor. It's in your own interest." Steve looked intently at the surgeon.

"We could also ask some patients and your assistants," Bob added.

"I'll check my calendar right away." Glassman reached over his desk for a leather-bound book. He leafed through the pages and nodded. "Well, I did surgery until the evening, then I went home to spend the evening with my wife, Melinda. I hope that helps you. If you don't have any more questions, I've got another meeting in ten minutes." He smiled apologetically at the detectives and looked at the door.

"We'll have to verify your story," Bob said, taking some notes.

"When was Sanders at your practice last Wednesday? We need to know when he arrived and when he left," Steve insisted.

"What has John Sanders to do with it?" The doctor looked annoyed, obviously losing his patience. Unwillingly he opened his diary again. "Here we go. John Sanders arrived at 2:00 p.m." He pointed to the entry on the page for September 4. "He was late because of a traffic jam. And he left at four, as far as I remember. Anything else?" Glassman got up and motioned them toward the door.

"Was Sanders alone when he visited you?" Bob relaxed in his armchair, giving Glassman the impression they weren't in a hurry.

Glassman said curtly, "No. Sanders was in the company of his lady. We had a meeting about a planned surgery. You know, only the best-looking girls get the best jobs, and I'm well known for my good work."

Steve looked over Bob's shoulder to read his notes. "What's the lady's name and address?" he asked.

Glassman looked annoyed. "I must ask my assistant." Still standing he dialed a number, waiting impatiently. "Debbie? I need the address of Gloria Thumbnail, John Sanders's lady. Can you check it for me? And give the gentlemen my private address as well." He waited, drumming his fingers on the polished desk surface. "You got it?" He listened and turned to Bob. "It's 1980 Pico Boulevard, in Culver City." He walked to the door and opened it. "That's it, I hope."

"One more question. Have you heard of Steps to Heaven?" Steve asked all of a sudden.

Dr. Glassman looked blank. Then a smile lit his handsome face. "Is it the new movie they are talking about everywhere?" He leaned against the wall, crossing his arms in front of him.

"Far from it," Steve said curtly.

"It's a new club in Culver City, which has a reputation for illegal drugs," Bob explained. "Have you been there with Sanders?"

"Don't know the place." Glassman shook his head. "Gentlemen, I'm sorry to disappoint you. As I said before, I'm a hard-working surgeon, and I wish I had more free time, but except for some golf on the weekends, you will find me here or in meetings and appointments with clients." Glassman checked his gold wristwatch. "Will you excuse me now? I have a great deal to do." He turned around and walked back to his desk.

"If you can think of anything more about John Sanders or Randolph Foreman, just give us a call at this number." Bob put a card printed with the phone number for the Culver City Police Department on the desk and stood up.

Dr. Glassman nodded. "Of course! Good-bye, Detectives." He rummaged in his desk, now ignoring them.

Debbie was not at her desk when Steve and Bob walked through the lobby. "Maybe she's painting her toenails?" Bob suggested.

At that moment she emerged from another room, smiling. "Here's the addresses you were asking for." She handed them a folded paper and accompanied them to the entrance door. "Have a nice day."

"Thank you, the same to you," Bob said.

"Bye!" Steve waved at Debbie as they left the practice.

"WE SHOULD check if there was a traffic jam like Sanders told us." Bob slumped in the passenger seat, unfolding the paper Debbie had given them.

"Yeah, later," Steve said, starting the car. "Do you think we should ask Glassman's wife about his alibi if they don't live far from here?"

"It's 790 Bolero Drive." Bob checked the GPS and nodded. "Let's do it right now."

"Okeydokey." Steve accelerated. He smiled with contentment when the Thunderbird sped up, and the engine roared.

"Stop! You went past the address!" Bob pointed at a large house behind them on the right.

Steve hit the brakes, the car coming to a squealing halt.

Bob inhaled deeply and got out of the Thunderbird. "Steve, you drive me nuts sometimes...."

"You deserve it." Steve chuckled. "Trust me, I have everything under control." He added, "I bet Glassman's wife will confirm his alibi."

"WHAT DID I tell you?" Steve looked at his watch. "It took three minutes to get her statement. Of course she agreed with her husband." Steve sighed, climbing in his car.

"No surprises," Bob said, fighting with the passenger door again. Steve leaned over to open the door from the inside.

Bob slid into the car. "Now to Bakersfield!"

"Can we stop by Christy's? It isn't far from here, and it won't take long." Steve raised his arm with the wristwatch to show Bob. "This damn watch is still a mystery to me."

"It's against regulations during an investigation. You'd better count that as dinner break," Bob said loftily.

"Dinner is on me, then. You choose the place. Okay?" Steve forced a grin.

Bob patted Steve's shoulder. "As long as you don't complain if Rollins finds out you did this on the city's dime."

"He won't know if you don't tell him," Steve said worriedly. Bob didn't say anything, keeping Steve on tenterhooks. Then he grinned, and Steve slapped him lightly on the knee. "Don't you dare!"

They drove out of Santa Barbara. On the outskirts Steve stopped the Thunderbird in front of a big mall. "You wanna come in with me, or do you prefer to sit outside watching girls?" he teased.

Bob was tempted to do just that, but he decided against it. He knew that Steve could spend hours at the jewelry store, checking out the watches.

"I'm coming." Bob swung his legs out of the car. "But do it quickly. It's after five. I don't want to get to Bakersfield too late. Maybe we can even talk to Enrico tonight and drive directly back home."

"Forget it. It'll take about two hours to get to Bakersfield." Steve locked the car. "I'm beat and want to get some rest. Looking at you, partner, it seems like you need a good night's sleep as well."

"I can't talk you out of this, can I?" Bob asked.

Steve reached up his hand to cup Bob's neck briefly. "You'll see, everything's going to be all right. Come on!" He tugged Bob into the mall. It was an enormous place, filled with happy shoppers and every sort of store. Soon Steve found the little jewelry store where he had bought his Yamamoto watch.

"What can I do for you, gentlemen?" A middle-aged man in a dark suit smiled at them from behind the counter at Christy's.

Steve fumbled to get his wristwatch off. "I bought this Yamamoto here and still don't know how to use some of its functions. For example, how does the alarm work?"

Bob smiled. He never understood why Steve was so fascinated with these modern watches offering some odd functions like moon phases. Bob just wanted a watch to show the exact time.

"Decide when you want the alarm to go off and turn the hands to that time. Push this button twice, and you'll hear a voice announce the time. Look, like this." The man took the watch, turned some buttons, and suddenly a voice proclaimed, "Attention, attention, it's six thirty."

"That's great!" Steve beamed at the man.

Bob looked around while the salesman was showing Steve the special functions of the watch.

"Thank you!" Finally Steve shook hands with the salesman.

"Now do you know how to use your magical watch?" Bob asked, looking over Steve's shoulder.

"Of course." Steve put on his watch proudly.

"You're welcome. Anything else I can do for you? A new watch for you as well?" The salesman took a silver watch out of the display case and offered it to Bob. "We have the newest creations by—"

"No, thanks, we're in a hurry." Bob propelled Steve out of the store. "Hey, I'm getting hungry, and you promised to buy me dinner."

"Coming right up!" Steve looked around. "Where do you want to eat?"

Bob noticed a little Chinese restaurant opposite the jewelry shop. "How about there? Some Cantonese chicken curry would be great."

"Why not?" Steve followed Bob to the restaurant. "I hope they have a spicy Peking soup. I love that stuff!"

Bob liked the quiet atmosphere inside the small restaurant. Steve had selected a table next to a big tank. "Look at those fish! Amazing colors, and do you think those corals are natural?" Steve stared at the tank, watching the exotic fish.

"Impressive," Bob admitted. The blue light from the aquarium gave the little restaurant a calming atmosphere.

Steve tore himself away from the sight and glanced through the menu. "I'll take a chop suey and my favorite soup. What about you?"

Bob rolled his eyes. "No Peking soup for me. Too spicy. But the chicken curry is okay. I do wonder about your stomach," he said, sipping the water the waitress brought over. "Someday you'll regret all these spicy foods."

"Keeps me healthy!" Steve rubbed his flat abdomen with a laugh.

They ate as quickly as possible, leaving the rest of the food on their plates.

Bob wanted to leave for Bakersfield before they got too sleepy. Luckily, at this time of the evening, they encountered little traffic. There was no direct route between the two cities, so Steve headed onto State Road 126 and over to Interstate 5 to get to their destination.

They arrived in Bakersfield about 9:00 p.m. and took the first exit off the highway to look for a motel room in the commercial area.

"Over there." Bob pointed at a one-story building. The entrance was illuminated with a large "Pink Flamingo." The light spilling out from the front window looked inviting.

Steve stopped the car right in front of the registration office and scrambled out of the car. "Finally!" he grumbled, waiting for Bob to get out of the passenger side.

"My feet are asleep," Bob complained, stretching his long legs carefully after the ride.

"Hope it's not too late to question Enrico!" Steve said, locking the car.

"Forget that." Bob looked at his watch. "It's past seven. Today we won't have a chance to meet Enrico. Let's get a room and plan the next day."

Reluctantly Steve agreed. Waiting for Bob to join him, he trudged to the entrance and pushed the door open.

The man behind the desk was reading a newspaper. He looked up when the bell over the door jingled.

"We need a double room for one night. How much is it?" Steve leaned on the counter.

"Sorry, no vacancy." The manager pointed to a sign behind him on the wall.

"Oh, no," Bob moaned. The idea of looking half the night for a motel room wasn't at all appealing. "It's the middle of the week!"

"There's a big convention in town. It lasts all week, and you won't find a single bed in Bakersfield, I'm sure," the man said.

Steve wiped his face and rubbed his eyes wearily.

Bob leaned heavily on the counter, next to Steve. "We are cops, always on duty to protect and serve," he said softly.

"Oh well, in that case, how can I help you?" the manager said, taking pity on them. He tapped his lips, thinking things over. "Listen, my brother is a cop, and I know how hard you guys work. My name's Sam, by the way."

"I'm Steve Randall, and this is my partner, Bob Curry."

"Wait, there's a little room, we just started to renovate. It has a bed and a sink, though. My assistant manager slept there the other night," Sam said with a frown. "It isn't comfortable at all, but it's the only thing I can come up with. Sorry."

Bob locked glances with his partner. *What a mess! I could be at home right now, getting my much-needed sleep. Instead you insisted on coming to this crazy town to speak to that weasel Enrico. You owe me, and not only dinner.*

Steve responded with an apologetic smile, squeezing Bob's arm. *I know. I'm a nut.*

Bob felt a strange sort of calm. Steve had the ability to defuse his anger with just a look and a smile. Partly convinced things would turn out right, Bob nodded reluctantly.

"Can you give us a special price, then?" Steve asked.

"Twenty dollars. And I'll throw in some bagels from the shop across the street for free!" Sam said.

"Okay, thanks, Sam. We'll take the room. Better than nothing." Bob picked up their bag.

Sam got up from his seat and pointed left down the long corridor. "It's at the end of the hall. Don't worry about the private sign." He shrugged. "I must have the key somewhere here." Sam rummaged in a drawer under his desk and came up with a large key. "Here you are."

He went with them to the room at the end of the corridor. "Be careful of the ladders. The painting isn't finished yet. I'll grab you some sheets for the bed and be back in a moment."

Bob unlocked the door and shoved it open. "Where's the light?" he mumbled.

Steve snaked his arm around him and found the switch. A small lamp stood on a little table next to an unmade single bed. The smell of new paint was strong but not completely unpleasant.

"You'll be happy in this room because there's a mop and a bucket over there. You could wash the floor for your supper," Bob joked. He looked around, taking in the paint cans and brushes. "We can still decide to drive home, can't we?" He was about ready to leave, but Steve held him back.

"Bob, it's only for one night. You take the bed, and I'll sleep in the car," Steve said, with a forced smile. "It's no big deal. You agreed to come with me to Bakersfield, and you deserve the best."

"The best?" Bob tossed a heavy dose of sarcasm into his reply and gave Steve the finger. "If this is the best, I don't want to know what is worse."

"Here's the linen." Sam came in with a blanket, a large sheet, a pillow, and a pillowcase. "Want me to make the bed?"

"I can do it, thanks," Bob answered. Steve waved jauntily as Sam walked back down the hall. "At least the sheets seem to be clean." Bob unfurled the bottom sheet and quickly tucked it in.

Steve sat down on a small wooden stool next to the bed. "About the sleeping arrangement...," he started, looking at Bob.

"Have a good night's sleep in your car," Bob said, hiding a smile.

"Yeah, see you in the morning." Steve fumbled for his car keys.

"Just kidding." Bob held his hand out and helped Steve up. "If you behave and don't hog all the space, we can try to share the bed." He waved at the neatly made bed. "Unless you really *want* to sleep in your beloved car." Bob smiled acidly.

"Okay. I promise to stay on my side." Steve exhaled, sounding relieved. "We can save some space if I sleep with my head at the bottom of the bed and you the other way around. When I was a kid, my cousins and I slept that way when we visited my Uncle George and Aunt Annie in New Jersey."

"That could work. I'm going to wash up." Bob opened their overnight bag and looked for the toothpaste, toothbrush, and a towel. With the supplies under his arm, he disappeared into the little bathroom.

When he returned, Steve had crawled into bed. He hadn't even changed into pajamas. He was wearing a T-shirt and boxers. Bob noticed that the paint cans now stood in a corner. Steve had put his jeans and shirt on the small stool, which was the only piece of furniture besides the bed.

"Hey, looks like home," Bob joked, shedding his cords and turtleneck. He got into bed with only his shorts on.

They arranged the blanket so they were covered. Bob looked at Steve's feet next to him and chuckled. "Buddy, I've never seen your feet so near. Which is the one you broke?"

"This one." Steve raised his left foot and braced himself on his elbow to look at Bob. "I was on the high school baseball team and tried to make it to home base, but I stumbled and fell. Lost the game! Nobody on the team liked me very much." He rolled his eyes over that teenage dilemma. "Since then my ankle seems weaker."

Without thinking Bob squeezed Steve's bad foot gently and covered both his feet with the blanket.

"Sleep tight," he said, reaching over to switch off the light. Snuggling into the pillow, he tried to get comfortable. As he was drifting off, he thought about the fact that he had a pillow, but Steve did not.

SOMETHING HIT Bob's nose, and he woke with a start. It was dark, and at first he had no idea where he was. The body writhing next to him brought him back to reality. He and Steve had crashed in the vacant room of the Pink Flamingo Motel in Bakersfield. And now Steve obviously had a problem.

"Buddy, what's wrong?" Bob sat up, looking at his restless partner. When Steve didn't react, Bob put a calming hand on his partner's back.

Steve struggled to get free of Bob's touch. "No, leave me alone. Can't stand it. Nooo!" he cried.

Bob turned 180 degrees until he lay beside his friend, cradling the shivering form in his arms. "It's nothing but a nightmare, buddy," he whispered, soothing Steve's trembling. "Shh, I'm right here. You can go to sleep again. Remember, tomorrow is an important day for us...." Bob said softly, wondering what Steve had dreamed about. He held Steve close until Steve calmed down and fell into a deeper sleep.

The last thought Bob had before he dozed off was that neither of them had a pillow now. He didn't retrieve it; he wanted to keep holding Steve to keep him asleep.

Chapter Seven

STEVE STRETCHED lazily, realizing that he was in the spare room in the motel on the outskirts of Bakersfield, awaiting Enrico's questioning. He snuggled deeper in the covers and felt another presence behind him. It was Bob, spooned up against him with his arm loosely on Steve's hip. Steve held his breath, very aware of the situation. The warmth of Bob next to him was cozy and wonderful. Steve didn't dare move, afraid of waking him. He savored the closeness.

At the same time, he wondered why Bob was lying head to head with him when they had gone to sleep lying in opposite directions. He looked at his watch. It was 6:00 a.m. Steve didn't want this moment to end, but he had to relieve his bladder.

Carefully he sat up, pushing his hands through his long hair. He grabbed his jeans from the stool and grinned. Bob's clothes were spread all over the floor. *Still the messy guy, huh?*

Bob moved, turning sluggishly onto his back. He began to snore lightly. Steve smiled at him. He was tempted to brush a thumb over the familiar cheek. He stopped halfway, chiding himself. What had once been a normal familiarity between them, underlining the closeness they'd always had, had turned into something more suspect. He shoved the disturbing thoughts aside and went into the bathroom.

Once he was dressed, Steve crossed the little entrance hall and went past the empty reception desk. Stepping outside he inhaled the fresh morning air. Today he hoped they would finally nail Enrico for the killing of Randolph Foreman. Steve could still see the fury and wounded pride in Enrico's eyes when he'd come into Randolph's office and found his lover with another man.

That night Randolph and Enrico must have had an argument that ended in Randolph's death. Steve almost felt responsible for the crime. If he hadn't fled the awkward situation, Randolph might still be alive.

If Bob had arrived earlier to pick Steve up, Enrico wouldn't have assumed his lover was cheating on him.

Steve decided to get the address of the local police headquarters into the GPS.

Returning to the motel, Steve saw a coffee vending machine, which was just the right thing to get Bob into action. With two steaming Styrofoam cups of coffee in his hands, Steve knocked on the door of their room. "Room service. Your breakfast, sir." When he heard no reaction, he knocked louder. "Bob, get up and open the damn door, the coffee is getting cold."

"Huh?" A sleepy Bob with tousled hair opened the door. "Sorry, I overslept. Have you busted Enrico already?" A slight grin tugged on the corners of his mouth. Bob took the cup out of Steve's hand and took a sip.

"Go on dreaming, partner. Seriously, I hope we get the interrogation done as quickly as possible. Then we'll head back to Culver City, write our reports, and that's it."

"What about the other cases, the drug-related deaths?" Bob finished his coffee, throwing the cup into the bin next to the door.

"Well, we'll take care of that next Saturday at the party Jessica told us about. I want to see her again." Steve almost growled, looking into his half-empty coffee cup to hide his confusion. Why did he keep getting so angry about Jessica assuming they were a couple? "I really want her to know the truth, and that I was attracted to her."

"Go ahead. No skin off my teeth," said Bob, putting on his shirt and pants. He grabbed his overnight bag when Steve pointed next to the bed. "Don't forget slipping into your boots." Bob made a face.

ONE HOUR later they sat in a small interrogation room at the police headquarters, waiting for Enrico Gonzales. He was currently the main suspect in the murder of his lover, Randolph Foreman. Steve tapped his feet on the wooden floor, unable to hide his nervousness. He was finally going to face the man who had probably killed Randolph in a jealous rage. Steve couldn't help feeling he was involved.

The door opened, and an officer led the suspect into the room.

"That's the murderer!" With a yell, Enrico tore away from the guard and lunged at Steve. Stunned, Steve lost his balance and fell over, along with his chair.

"Shut up!" It took Bob and the other officer a moment to keep the furious man at bay. With all their strength, they bent his arms backward and held him tight. "You've just assaulted a police officer! That will be added on to the charges against you!" Bob forced Enrico down into his chair and handcuffed him to the table. Enrico tried to resist, then gave up.

Enrico stared at Steve. "He's a cop? I was sure that he murdered Randy!"

Bob looked at Steve. "Everything okay?"

"You bet!" Steve hissed, inspecting the broken chair leg before he hit the wall with the leg.

"I didn't mean to hurt a cop," Enrico said. "I've got nothing to do with Randolph's death."

"Do we have another chair for my partner?" Bob looked at the officer.

The man nodded. "In the other office," he said, pointing to the door.

Bob stood up, positioning himself next to the suspect while the officer went to get another chair.

Steve bent over the desk, his gaze piercing Enrico. "What you just did will cost you, asshole. You're the main suspect in the killing of Randolph Foreman." He leaned back, pretending to assess Enrico's worth. "You have waived your right to have an attorney present, and anything you say can and will be used against you. Let's summarize. You came into Foreman's studio looking for him on Tuesday, September 3 and saw me there. You were beside yourself with rage, so what did you do?"

"Believe me, when I heard of Randy's death, I remembered seeing you with him in the studio. I thought it was you who...." Enrico shook his head before he went on. "The two of you were kissing!" Now he yelled, rage visible in his dark eyes.

"Tell me what happened after I left the photo studio!" Steve insisted. "Did you have an argument with Mr. Foreman, your lover?"

"*Ex*-lover." Enrico emphasized the first syllable. "I split up with him shortly before and only went back because he owed me some pay." He curled his lip at Steve. "I never expected him to take comfort with another guy so quickly." His eyes darkened, and his voice softened. "Maybe I reacted too quickly, seeing Randy with another man, but after I had my money, he kept whining about a lost love." Enrico shook his head. "So I left him and didn't hear from him again. Then I read the news about his death."

The officer appeared with a chair, and Bob took it from him. "Thanks."

Steve sat down, feeling disillusioned all of a sudden. All his assumptions were going up in smoke.

"Where were you last Tuesday night, September 3, and the following morning?" Bob butted in, taking out his notepad.

"I left Randy's place at eight, maybe, and drove to Tony's right away," Enrico explained.

"Who's Tony?" Steve asked.

"Tony is my boyfriend. He can attest that I was with him all night and the next day. I'm sorry that Randy is dead, but I have nothing to do with it. When I saw you here in the police department—" He looked at Steve remorsefully. "I thought the police had busted the murderer, and I got carried away. Sorry."

"What is Tony's full name and address?" Steve asked curtly, giving his pen to Bob.

"Anthony Burke, 650 Bernard Street, here in Bakersfield," Enrico said tightly.

"So why did you leave town in a rush?" Bob asked, scribbling in his notepad. "Your landlady saw you carrying a suitcase."

"To get back to my boyfriend," Enrico said petulantly. "Tony is such a lovable boy, and he promised me a great career in New York. Compared to him, Randy was a bore. He was always afraid to try new things, to take a risk in life."

"Why did you get involved with him if you thought he was such a bore?" Bob looked up.

Enrico shrugged. "We met on a photo shoot. I knew he had a good reputation, and I was the lucky guy who got the cover for *GQ*."

"When was that?" Steve wanted to know.

"Let me think about it." Enrico looked thoughtful. "Must've been three or four months ago, early summer."

"Okay, you two became a couple after the cover shoot," Bob said. "And then?"

Enrico cleared his throat. "Randy needed someone to take care of him. He was so vulnerable and sweet. I couldn't resist."

"That's all well and good, but it didn't last. Why not?" Steve asked, leaning forward in his chair.

"Randy was so moody and sometimes depressed. I couldn't stand it any longer." Enrico moved his hands nervously, the handcuffs clanking against the table.

"Any idea why he was depressed?" Bob had stopped writing.

"He didn't want to talk about it, but I got the impression something was bothering him."

"And now he's dead," Bob stated dryly.

"Can you think of any enemies Randolph might have had?" Steve asked.

"You see, Randy always fell for boys who didn't really care for him in the end. When we met, I was having a hard time too." Enrico rubbed his hands nervously. "We were there for each other, and I appreciated our relationship. But after a while...." He paused. "I needed someone different. Tony offered me what I needed. When I told Randy about my new love, he went nuts, got even more depressed, and didn't want to let go." He looked up with a shrug. "Maybe he found somebody else and went overboard. Pestered him with his out-of-control tendencies."

"So you say that you have an alibi for that evening until the following morning, and you didn't see anyone else when you left Randy's studio that evening," Steve said wearily.

"No, but I remember that Randy talked about a meeting with his boss, Sanders. I didn't care, to be honest." Enrico sighed, looking at his fingers. Then he brightened with a hopeful expression. "Can I go now? I have nothing to do with Randy's murder. Tony is waiting to take me to the East Coast. A new producer is casting a movie, and I am up for the part."

"You'll have to stay with Tony here in Bakersfield," Steve said. Gonzales looked annoyed. "You'll have to be available in case we have some more questions for you and Tony. We need to know exactly where you will be at all times until this case is solved. You won't be able to leave the state until your name is cleared," Bob said sternly. "You aren't off the suspect list so easily."

"But wait!" Enrico tried to get up. "I could get a part in a real movie. I have to make money."

"Sorry," Steve said, very tired of the whole case. "There'll be another time. If Tony is outside, then we need to verify your alibi."

"He's at home, not here. Damn," Enrico said, slumping in the chair. "I had a chance there!"

"Do you know a club called Steps to Heaven?" Bob asked.

Steve sent him an appreciative glance. *Good question, buddy. I almost forgot about it.*

"Yeah, it's the premiere place for people who want to climb the ladder of success." Enrico smiled for the first time. "There's a fantastic atmosphere, lights, glamour, the whole thing. The DJ is first class—lots of the latest bands and music." He swayed as if listening to an inner beat. "Tony made a real difference in my life. I met him there. Nothing can compete with Steps to Heaven."

"When was the last time you were there?" Steve perked up. Maybe this was the break they needed.

Enrico hesitated. "I met Tony at the club maybe three weeks ago. Since then we've spent every Saturday night there."

"What about last weekend? Tell us about your visit to the club. Anything memorable? We know that you can get drugs there. Did you attend one of those parties?" Steve asked.

"How do you know?" Enrico looked irritated.

"We have our sources," Bob added. "Are you a user or a pusher?"

"No, not at all!" Enrico's face reddened. "I knew there were parties in the back rooms, and rumors said you could get good stuff there."

"And you didn't even try Blue Rocket?" Steve spilled out.

Enrico shook his head. "That's horrible stuff! Tony tried it once, and he felt terribly sick afterward."

"Do you know if Randolph Foreman took any drugs?" Bob exchanged glances with Steve.

"No. He acted like a freak when people mentioned Blue Rocket or other drugs. As I said, Randy didn't take risks. A bore…."

"Can you tell us about the owner of the club? Who is behind the business?" Steve got more interested with every minute. Maybe Randolph's death had to do with the club.

"That's one of the many secrets. Nobody has seen the boss of the establishment. Tony told me the bartender is an important man. He regulates when there's a back-room party and who is allowed to join."

"Has Randolph ever been to the club? What do you think?" Bob had stopped scribbling.

"I don't believe so. He didn't like the fuss about that establishment. I really can't help you. Randy and I split up, and whoever killed him should be found quickly. Randy didn't deserve to die this way." Enrico leaned back, exhausted. "You have a smoke for me?" he asked sheepishly, rattling his cuffed wrists.

"Maybe later," Bob said curtly, putting his notepad in his pocket.

"We'll talk to the officer in charge, and you will be released shortly. And don't go out of state," Steve reminded him, walking to the door to let the officer in.

Enrico was uncuffed, then Bob gave him a form to sign signifying that he knew his rights and had participated willingly in the interrogation. "You can go now. We'll get your statement typed up, and then you can return at your convenience to sign it officially."

STEVE AND Bob left the Bakersfield police headquarters in silence. Sitting in the car, Bob said, "We should ask Tony about Enrico's alibi, but I have the feeling Enrico has nothing to do with Randolph's death."

"You could be right, but I'm not letting him off the hook so easily," Steve admitted, starting the car. "Off to Tony Burke's. Pull my notebook out of my jacket pocket, would you? I wrote down the address."

Bob leaned over and slid his hand into Steve's leather jacket, fumbling in the pocket.

"Hey, do you want me to drive into a wall? I'm ticklish, you know." Steve squirmed in his seat, trying to avoid Bob's hand.

"Calm down, I got it." Bob grinned and opened the pad. "Tony Burke. Never heard of him. Must not be famous yet." He waited for the GPS to give the direction. "Turn right at the next street," a friendly female voice told them.

Steve had to take a sudden sharp turn. Bob bumped into him, his sunglasses sliding down his nose.

"Hey, what're you thinking?" Bob complained, readjusting his glasses.

"There's a seat belt," Steve scolded. Bob often forgot to fasten his belt.

"Okay, but your driving skills are unnerving. The last thing we need is to be stopped by a traffic cop," Bob complained, but there was a lightness in his voice.

Steve hoped that their easy banter and renewed ease with each other would brighten the day, despite all the troubles waiting for them.

"Here we are," Steve said, impressed by the mansion flanked by huge trees. "Obviously Mr. Burke lives upper class. Look at the large windows, and I bet there's an Olympic-sized pool in the back." He grinned at Bob and got out of the car. *Being in the modeling business can't be such a bad life.* He snorted, thinking of his own photo shoot. *I'll stick with my day job.*

Steve and Bob crossed the lawn and rang the bell. Nothing happened. Steve was about to try it again when he heard steps from inside the mansion. The door opened partway. A middle-aged man in a white shirt and cut-off jeans was standing in the hallway, eyeing them suspiciously.

"Yeah?" He blew a strand of ash-blond hair off his forehead, examining them carefully with dark gray eyes.

"Are you Anthony Burke? We're Detectives Steve Randall and Bob Curry, Culver City Police. May we come in?"

When there was no immediate reaction, Bob pulled out his badge and repeated, "Are you Anthony Burke?" He took a step forward.

"Yes, I'm Anthony Burke. Of course, Officers, you can come in," Burke said as if coming out of a trance. "What's your visit about?"

"We've some questions regarding the death of Randolph Foreman last Tuesday night." Steve looked past the man into the interior of the house.

"Randolph Foreman? I didn't know him personally, but a friend of mine did. This way, please."

Tony led them through a dark hall into a room overlooking the large garden. Steve suppressed a whistle, seeing an Olympic-sized pool, just as he'd joked about, with a small pavilion set up like a bar. There were canvas chairs and round tables on one side and chaise lounges on the other.

"You have a nice home," Bob said, looking around the expensive décor.

"Sorry, it's messy. I'm getting ready for a trip to New York and have some stuff to pack and arrange." Tony grabbed some clothes off the couch and picked up a full ashtray to take it out of the room. "Have a seat. I'll be right back." He gave a distracted smile and hurried down the corridor.

"I wouldn't object to living here." Steve sank into the soft cushions of the couch, gesturing to Bob to sit beside him.

"Something about the man makes me nervous, I don't know why," Bob said in a low voice, joining him.

"I bet he's nervous too, having two cops at his place," Steve said. A loud rumbling of his stomach made him sit straighter. "Remind me that I need something to eat soon."

"What about stopping at Dinah's when we get back to Culver City?"

Steve checked his watch and nodded. "Once we're done here, we can buy some donuts. Then we'll head straight back to Culver City. We can make it just in time to be at the diner for a late lunch."

"Okay, okay," Bob agreed. "I hope Tony is cooperative, and you can have your stomach filled soon."

Tony entered the room and rubbed his hands. He came to a halt in front of the coffee table. "What do you want to know? I didn't know Randy, and I have no idea why...."

"Just tell us where you were last Tuesday night and Wednesday," Steve said, pulling out his own notepad.

Tony ran his hand over his head, finger combing his hair. "Mm, let me think... last Tuesday? I had that date with Mizzie, and later...." He frowned. "Is this an interrogation? Do you suspect me of being involved in a crime? My God, that's unbelievable!" Tony rubbed his hands again, and Steve noticed he was trembling. The man was irritated.

"It's just routine," Bob said in a soft voice, and Tony relaxed visibly. "We have to ask if someone can swear to where you were on Tuesday and Wednesday."

Tony Burke paused before he said, "I was with Mr. Gonzales. We're business partners and had some projects to discuss. Yesterday, Enr—Mr. Gonzales was arrested." Tony looked uncomfortable and tired. "It's such a mess...."

"When exactly did Mr. Gonzales arrive at your place last Tuesday?" Steve asked, ready to write the needed information.

"That's difficult." Again, Tony paused. "Wait. I made dinner and had to wait for him. It must have been about ten when he arrived. Is that all?"

"Not yet," Bob said, sitting up straighter. "Can anyone prove that you were together? Maybe you went out?"

"No, after dinner we watched some TV and spoke about our plans," Tony said.

"Randolph Foreman was killed in the night from Tuesday to Wednesday. We'll check your alibi," Bob said.

"And what about Wednesday morning and afternoon?" Steve butted in.

Tony frowned. "As far as I remember, we had breakfast in Burger King. And in the afternoon... we did some shopping. I don't know if that helps." Tony looked from Steve to Bob with a hopeful expression.

"Thank you, Mr. Burke. In case you have some more useful information regarding Mr. Foreman's death, don't hesitate to call the

CCPD. Here's our number." Steve stretched his hand out and got a card from Bob, which he handed over to Burke.

He and Bob stood up and shook hands with Tony Burke, who still looked uncomfortable.

Leaving the large room, Steve turned to Tony. "Mr. Burke, you met Enrico Gonzales at Steps to Heaven. What is it that makes that club so special?"

"Huh? What club?" Tony stopped, tapping his bottom lip. "Ah, you mean the club for young actors, photographers, and models hoping to become famous one day." He laughed. "It's the latest thing in Culver City and will be well known everywhere in California." He led them to the door. "I hope I helped. Bye."

"Is the club so famous because of Blue Rocket?" Bob probed, watching Tony's reaction.

"I have no idea what you're talking about." Tony paled.

Steve noticed Tony's hands tremble on the doorknob. "We know that Blue Rocket is a new drug available at Steps to Heaven. And we know you've taken it," Steve said, staring intently at him. He knew how to break a man.

"I'm no junkie, no way!" Tony raised his voice, breaking the eye contact. "I mean, I tried that stuff once, and it didn't have the desired effect on me."

"What are the desired effects of Blue Rocket?" Bob asked, leaning against the door. "How did it make you feel?"

Tony took a long breath. "Normally you take Blue Rocket and feel energetic and full of confidence. You are powerful and don't need a lot of sleep. And your heartbeat races. That was my problem."

"What happened?" Steve looked at Tony. Underneath his elegant facade, he looked fragile and not at all healthy.

"I have a cardiac defect. Not the best condition to take Blue Rocket." Tony sighed.

"What do you know about other side effects?" Steve pulled out his notepad again.

Tony nodded. "A friend of a friend injected the stuff and collapsed. I've heard of others who took Blue Rocket for a longer time, and they suffered from panic attacks."

"Did you inject the drug yourself?" Bob asked, tensing.

"No. I was offered a pill. Bad enough." Tony looked remorseful.

"Could anybody get the drug at the club?" Steve looked up from writing.

"Oh, no. Another member has to recommend you. The first pill you get is free, then you have to pay." Tony paused. "I always wondered why only members got it. And it was affordable."

"Maybe the pushers were still testing the stuff and needed some members acting unwittingly as guinea pigs," Steve said.

"Who introduced you to the drug? Any names would be helpful," Bob said.

Tony shook his head. "I don't remember any names, except Juan the bartender and DJ Ronnie. I had to fill in a membership card, though. They wanted to make the backroom parties something special that only invited members could join."

"Have you heard about the drug-related deaths in the last few months? Blue Rocket was the reason for at least six deaths," Steve said.

"Yes, I heard. It's time to find out who is responsible for all those overdose victims," Tony said with conviction. "Let me repeat—I have nothing to do with Blue Rocket." He reached around Bob to open the door. "If you need to, don't hesitate to call me. For the next week, I'll be in New York, though."

"We have to ask you to stay in town until we have checked your and Mr. Gonzales's alibis," Bob said, stepping out of the house.

"What? How can you restrict my movements? I had nothing to do with the case! This trip could be an important step in my career, and Enrico's too," Tony Burke said indignantly.

"It looks as if you don't have to worry about money," Steve said, referring to the large mansion.

"It's my father's," Tony said. "Inform me immediately when I can leave the state, so I can change my travel plans."

"We'll let you know if we need you again." Bob smiled at Tony Burke, and Steve shook his hand.

BACK IN the car, Steve tapped his fingers on the steering wheel and looked at Bob. "If you ask me, Enrico didn't murder Randolph. He had no motive to kill his ex-lover. He's happy with Tony Burke, and their alibis sound believable."

"Maybe we're approaching this murder all wrong. We've struck out on all the obvious suspects," Bob said, rummaging in the compartment for some candy. Unwrapping a peppermint for himself and one for Steve, he said suddenly, "That's it! I know what was wrong with Tony! Did you see his eyes? The pupils were dilated. Either he was high or he's on some powerful painkillers...."

"Really?" Steve frowned. He thought back, picturing Tony in his mind. "I only noticed that his hands were trembling. I thought it was because he was nervous, but you could be right. He's really a big fan of Steps to Heaven. Do you think he's involved in the drug trade there? Does his money really come from his father? Think of the big house, the garden...."

"Might be, I'm not sure." Bob chewed noisily on his peppermint candy.

"Do you mind?" Steve opened his mouth while concentrating on turning left at the corner.

Bob shoved another candy between Steve's lips. "You're such a spoiled ass." He smiled. "Maybe this has to do with the club," he said seriously. "We may be working on one big case instead of two. So many loose threads lead back to Steps to Heaven."

Steve sighed. "Bob, we've got to get back to Culver City and write up these statements, see if anything more has turned up from forensics."

"I told you it would be wiser to wait until Enrico was in our fair city." Bob crumpled the candy wrappers.

"Maybe you're right," Steve admitted, accelerating the car. The trip had been a bust. But they'd managed to talk to three suspects in the case in less than two days and been able to spend time together too.

Steve sighed again, leaning his elbow out the window of the Thunderbird.

Bob put a hand on Steve's thigh, squeezing gently. "We're fairly certain that Enrico wasn't involved, and we can concentrate on other suspects. We still have to question Randy's other friends and relatives," Bob said. "And I should call Linda. She worked with him several times. She may have insight into his behavior and his relationship with Enrico and Chris Barber, not to mention anyone else we haven't turned up yet."

Steve patted Bob's hand. "We should also check on some other alibis. For example, Sanders's girlfriend, Gloria What's-her-name." Steve took a left a little too fast, and the tires squealed.

Bob caught his breath. "Sanders said he was with her all night, and on Wednesday they went to Santa Barbara to see Dr. Glassman. I'm going to call her when we're back at the precinct."

When Steve and Bob finally arrived at Dinah's diner, it was past lunchtime. They had a quick soup and salad without seeing Bella or Jessica.

"Isn't Jessica at work today?" Steve asked when Jane, another waitress, brought the bill.

"No, it's Jessica's day off," Jane explained. "Can I do anything else for you?"

"No, thanks," Bob smiled, putting a bill on the table.

"Thanks so much, and have a wonderful day!" Jane beamed at Bob.

"Sure, wonderful work," Steve grumbled, strutting to the door.

"HEY, LONG time no see," Officer Simon said, offering a false smile when they walked down the hall to their office.

"Hope you haven't missed us too much." Steve snorted.

"I bet he has," Bob joked without humor.

They entered the squad room and walked to their desks.

Steve had just sat down when the door opened, and Rollins came in, some folders under his arm.

Putting on his winning smile, Steve began, "Lieutenant, good to see you back. How are—"

"Stop buttering me up, Randall!" Rollins bellowed, opening the door to his office. "Come in!"

His face was darker than usual, from annoyance. He had several folders in front of him on his desk and opened the first one. "I'm working my way through the reports and see you've been in Bakersfield to interrogate Enrico Gonzales." Rollins looked at them. The expression on his face didn't promise anything good.

"We were sure we had Randolph Foreman's murderer in custody and needed to ask him some important questions." Bob went quiet, and Steve briefly put his hand on Bob's back.

"Who ordered this assignment?" Rollins wanted to know.

"I wanted to find out if the Bakersfield cops actually had Randolph's murderer in custody," Steve explained.

"That's not an answer to my question." Rollins's anger was palpable. "Wasn't Lieutenant Copperfield in charge of leading this office during my absence?" Rollins snapped.

"Yes, and we called him," Bob said quietly.

"Sorry, we should have called you too, before we left," Steve said with remorse. "At least the trip wasn't in vain. We ruled out a suspect and got alibis on people."

Rollins leaned back and sighed. "It's the last time I tolerate such a performance." He waved them out.

At the door Bob turned around. "Sir, there's another thing we have to tell you."

"What is it?" Rollins looked up from the folder.

Bob cleared his throat. "We have a good lead on that new place, Steps to Heaven, and we want to go undercover to a party Saturday to get info on Blue Rocket."

"And what's the catch?" Rollins frowned.

"No catch. I'll go in as an up-and-coming photographer." Steve held up a pretend camera.

"I'll be an out-of-work model," Bob said.

"If you have good leads on this Blue Rocket and can tie it back to Steps to Heaven, then go undercover and check out the club." Rollins took a pen and a paper. "I need the address and the time you'll be there."

"Of course, sir." Steve went to the door, opening it for Bob to go first.

"We'll give you all the information on our assignment at the club," Bob added and went out. Steve followed, closing the door after him with a light kick.

"I'm glad Rollins approves of our plan." Bob sat down behind his desk, turning on his computer.

"The boss is on our side." Steve nodded.

The rest of the day, they did paperwork, making up for the time they had been out of town.

Chapter Eight

BOB PUT the receiver down and leaned back in his chair, stretching his legs and crossing his arms behind his neck.

"I'm all ears. What did Linda tell you? I couldn't make any sense out of 'Yeah, really, huh' and other nonsense sounds," Steve complained while chewing on a pencil.

Bob exhaled and sat up straighter. "First of all, Linda says hi to you. She's sorry that you got into trouble because of Randy."

"I appreciate her concern," Steve said, leaning forward. "Fire away! What else did she say?"

Bob opened the folder on Randolph's case. "Linda confirms what others have said about Randolph. He was up one minute, down the next, struggling with his need to find the love of his life, and people used his reputation as an esteemed artist. So nothing new. But Linda told me that Randolph was friends with a model who joined Steps to Heaven shortly after they met at the studio."

Steve whistled. "Let me guess. Randolph fell in love with this new model. This mysterious boyfriend had enough of him and killed him."

"Hold your horses and listen," Bob chided. "Linda says his name was something like Evan. Randolph and Evan had planned to do a project together, but Evan was found dead."

"When?" Steve tensed, moving the pencil restlessly in his hands.

Bob gathered his thoughts and said, "Must've happened months ago. Linda remembers Randolph being out of his mind when the coroner found out there was an amphetamine in Evan's body. Since Evan's death Randy had been sad and depressed, obviously unable to cope with his friend's death."

Steve nodded. "That makes sense. But he didn't act as if he were on the edge when I was there. Sure, he seemed like he needed someone."

"Linda said that he even talked about taking revenge on whoever was responsible for the death of his friend," Bob said, looking at Steve with a frown. "Obviously he suspected someone at the club was spreading bad drugs. That's it." Bob shut the folder and drank from his half-empty coffee mug. "It's cold." He made a face.

"Another needless death to add to the list. Now we know why Randolph wanted to speak with us and offered to be an informant. He had a personal interest in uncovering what was going on at Steps to Heaven. But we were too late." Steve threw the pencil across the table, frustrated. It dropped into Bob's lap, and Bob doubled over in faked agony.

"Any damage to important parts?" A little smile crept over Steve's face.

Bob gave him the finger and tossed back the pencil.

"Is this where I'm supposed to be?" A young woman with blonde hair and wearing a short skirt stood in the doorway, looking around indecisively.

Bob could have kicked himself. Flipping Steve the bird just as a lady entered the squad room was very unprofessional.

"Can we help you? What's your name?" Steve asked politely.

"I was told to be here at nine," she said, twisting her purse strap around her fingers. "My name is Gloria Thumbnail, and John Sanders is my boyfriend. You need to ask me some questions?"

Steve pulled out a chair. "Sit down, please."

Gloria sat down, looking from Steve to Bob. "I don't know why I have to be here. John told me about the terrible death of one of his best photographers." She sniffed. "I knew Randolph. He was such a lovely person." Gloria took out a hanky from her purse and blew her nose.

"It's just routine," Bob said to calm her. "Where were you last Tuesday and Wednesday?"

"I was with John. I waited for him at his place because he had a meeting with some of his employees. Then we spent the night together and went to Santa Barbara the next day to see Dr. Glassman."

"You have a remarkable memory," Steve said. "Ask me what I had for dinner last night, and I couldn't tell you."

Gloria blushed. "We see each other every Wednesday, and I was looking forward to meeting Dr. Glassman the next day. So it's no big deal remembering last Wednesday."

"Did John Sanders react differently than the other times you saw each other? I mean, when he came home on Tuesday evening?" Bob asked.

"John is the gentlest man I have ever met," Gloria said with conviction.

"That isn't the answer to our question," Steve said harshly.

Gloria swallowed. "Thinking about it, I have to admit, he looked tired, nothing unusual for him, though." She fumbled with the hanky. "He often works more than ten hours a day."

Bob butted in. "Gloria, we need you to sign a statement verifying your whereabouts on the night of Tuesday, September 3 and all day Wednesday, September 4, and who you were with."

"And tell the truth. Perjury is a crime, punishable by time in jail," Steve said seriously, leaning forward in his chair. "We need to verify everyone's alibis for that night when Randolph Foreman was killed. So, were you with Sanders all the time?"

Gloria nodded, her face pale.

Bob got the feeling she was hiding something. He locked eyes with Steve. "Gloria, tell us the truth. You weren't with Sanders, were you?" Bob said in a soft voice.

Gloria crumpled the hanky in her hands. "Yes, I was with John, but I had to wait for him longer than usual. I had expected him to be at his place about 11:00 p.m. I knew he had a meeting, and sometimes they drink at the bar, so I wasn't worried." Gloria looked up.

"But John didn't show up," Steve stated. "When did he come home?"

"I must have fallen asleep. I woke up hearing him rummaging around in the bedroom. I asked him where he had been, and he was very attentive, apologizing." She shrugged. "He told me he and Chris, his assistant, met another businessman, and he forgot about the time. That's all. On Wednesday we went to see Dr. Glassman."

Steve regarded her sternly. "Who was the other businessman? Did John give any explanation?"

"Not really. He seemed really pleased about the meeting on Tuesday and looked forward to discussing further plans with Dr. Glassman." Gloria sounded exhausted.

"What kind of plans did he have in mind?" Bob looked at her intently.

Gloria cleared her throat. "Some big deal with a company from the East Coast. But he never involves me in his plans."

"So why did you accompany him to visit Dr. Glassman?" Bob asked.

Gloria blushed. "John promised to ask Dr. Glassman about me having plastic surgery." She blushed even more.

"Really? Why?" Bob looked at the young woman, puzzled.

Steve leaned forward in his chair. "What kind of surgery did you want?"

Bob would have liked to kick Steve's ass for such a personal question, but on the other hand, he was interested to know why a pretty young woman would want plastic surgery.

"I have the chance to be in his next photo shoot. The new generation of models. But, you know...." She looked down at herself, obviously not content with her body.

"I have no idea," Steve said.

Gloria coughed. "It's my midsection." She pushed a little on her nearly flat belly. "I hope that's all you need to know." She put her hanky back in her purse and shifted on her chair.

"Gloria, thank you for your statement. We'll have it typed up, and you'll have to return to sign it officially." Steve stood up and shook her hand.

Bob went to open the door for her, ushering the young woman out of the room.

"She wants to have plastic surgery? She looks great to me." Steve shook his head.

"I can't believe that either. But back to business. Obviously, Sanders's alibi isn't airtight. We have to question him again." Bob opened a new document on his computer.

"Can't we take a break?" Steve groaned, peering into his empty coffee cup. "It's dinnertime. I need something to fill me up."

Bob opened the big folder containing the unsolved drug-related deaths from the last six months. What did they have in common? All the victims had worked in the fashion industry, most as models. All had been ambitious young people. The crime lab technicians had found an unknown cocktail of amphetamines in each body.

Flipping over a page in the report for a young victim, Caren Schmidt, Bob caught sight of a close-up picture of her arms. He searched through the other files, coming up with crime photos of Mike Jones and Deedee Marie. He whistled, lining up the pictures.

"Look, Steve! All the victims of drug overdoses had injection marks on their bodies. It looks as if they injected the stuff."

Steve stopped writing a report. "I can imagine Randolph going crazy when he found out that his good friend—possibly lover—had been found dead, killed by an unknown drug." Steve ran his hand through his hair. "Could Evan have taken Blue Rocket? Or did Evan die like so many other junkies, from an overdose of heroin or cocaine? You want me to look for Evan's records?" Steve asked. "All you have to do is finish my last report. Be kind and help an overworked friend."

Bob couldn't resist Steve's charms. Wordlessly he came around the table to take care of the half-written report.

"What do I owe you?" Steve stood up, squeezing Bob's hand.

Bob shrugged. "I'm halfway through the folder and haven't found anyone called Evan. The last names are sorted alphabetically. Maybe you'll find him under X." Bob shoved the big folder across the desk.

Steve grabbed it, grunted something under his breath, and went to work, checking the remaining reports of the eight drug-related deaths since spring.

Suddenly he snorted. "That's it! Evan Porter, found dead May sixteenth, four months ago. His landlady found him lying lifeless in his apartment. It looked as if he'd had a heart attack."

"A heart attack? And no drugs involved?" Bob shook his head and went on typing.

"Listen carefully, partner." Steve read on, "The autopsy revealed that he had traces of a drug similar to cocaine in his bloodstream that had probably caused his death. By the sound of it, Evan was one of the earliest deaths from Blue Rocket. The crime lab hadn't figured out the actual compound of the drug back then." Steve kicked Bob under the table. "Hey, you hear me?"

"Yeah, loud and clear. I heard that they are still searching for the exact compound of Blue Rocket, but it seems to belong to the group of amphetamines." Bob finished typing the report and printed it out. "I can't wait to investigate at Steps to Heaven next Saturday."

"Did Millie find out about the owner?" Steve asked.

"Wait a sec." Bob opened the folder again, leafing through the pages. "It says that Steps to Heaven belongs to Entertainment Corporation, whoever that is." He shrugged.

"Maybe we'll learn more when Jessica gets us into that party," Steve said.

Bob caught his eye. "I know you're uncomfortable going as a gay couple, but it's just for one night."

Steve's face lit up. "Okay. I'll take my camera and pretend to be an up-and-coming photographer. You're a model looking for a profitable job." He framed his fingers like a fashion photographer.

"Whoa, what about the other way around?" Bob waved his hand as if erasing the picture Steve was creating. "*You are* the model, and you have experience already," Bob said in his most convincing voice. "In fact, maybe we can get some of the pictures Randolph took of you to pass around as your portfolio."

"I don't want to be reminded of that photo session," Steve said sourly. Then his mood brightened. "Larry could lend you his satin pants, the green ones," Steve said enthusiastically. "With your black shirt, you'd look like a hot star. All the photo agencies would want to snap you up."

Bob knew that Larry, the owner of Larry's pub, loved flashy clothes. More than once they had teased him that he could be a disco dancer. "I doubt that." Bob tried to imagine himself in such an outfit. He shook his head. "Forget about it, partner. *I* am the photographer, and you are the model. We can put a lot of gel in your hair, like Randolph did."

Steve looked embarrassed, and Bob realized he had made a mistake. Steve was probably still feeling vulnerable about the whole situation. Changing his tactics, Bob lowered his voice almost to a whisper and leaned in to speak into Steve's ear. "I agree, on one condition. I choose my outfit, okay?"

Steve looked relieved. He nodded. "No objections here. You'd look a tad overdressed in Larry's pants anyway. What about discussing the matter this evening? The beer is on me."

"It's a deal." Bob looked at the clock on the wall over Rollins's office door. "Let's hurry up with the reports. We're off soon."

Reluctantly Steve turned back to work, poring over the case files. The next two hours were only interrupted by a walk to the bathroom or, in Steve's case, an extra visit to the candy machine.

"Finally!" Steve bundled the sheets in front of him and put them in the stack. "What about you?"

Bob was just printing out the last arrest report. "Considering that I rewrote one of your reports as well, I'll be finished in a minute," he teased gently.

Bob felt tired. He would have preferred to go straight home after work, but he didn't want to disappoint Steve. Steve obviously needed to talk about the case and the upcoming party at Steps to Heaven.

As they headed north to Steve's place, Bob had an idea. "Why not have dinner at Larry's pub? Larry might have the latest news off the street and could give us a couple of names of people to talk to at the party."

"Sounds like a plan. I'm in the mood for a game of pool."

Bob gave him a little smile. "I'm not asking him about those green pants, though."

Steve looked at him with those intense blue eyes, and Bob surrendered to the affection reflected on his face. Despite their different opinions about cars and food, they were unbeatable as a team.

"YOUR WISH was my command." Steve shut the motor off and was about to get out of the Thunderbird.

Startled, Bob realized he had daydreamed for the entire trip from the police station.

"Here we are at Larry's pub. Come on, partner."

"Okay, okay…. Damn door!" Bob struggled to open it.

"Hey, take it easy. My precious car needs a general overhaul." Steve reached over to rub Bob's back.

Bob felt Steve's hand there and suppressed a sigh. *So good.* Not for the first time, Bob wondered how a simple word or touch could make him feel so much better. For a moment he leaned into the warmth, savoring the familiar closeness.

Then they got out of the car and walked into their friend's bar, the cigarette smoke and babble of voices surrounding them like a familiar cloud. Bob went over to their favorite place at the end of the bar, where it wasn't too noisy.

A man dressed in black emerged from the kitchen, juggling a tray laden with burgers and fries.

"Larry, how did you know? That's just what we were waiting for, weren't we, Bob?" Steve nudged Bob in the side.

"Exactly. And a salad for me—without onions." Bob made himself comfortable on the stool.

"Hey, guys, where have you been all this time?" Larry set down the tray and clasped hands with them.

"Don't ask, Larry," Steve sighed and snatched some fries from the plate. "Linda Thornton's photographer Randolph Foreman was murdered last Tuesday. We haven't gotten any further in the case."

Larry nodded. "The modeling biz is risky. What about the drug-related deaths? Didn't you mention they were models and wannabe actors? Are there any similarities?" He put the loaded tray on the table.

Bob bent forward, lowering his voice. "You've heard about the new drug on the street? All the recent victims had Blue Rocket in their bloodstreams. That drug is dangerous. It has a deadly amphetamine compound, which the lab has only partially analyzed. We have to find the people responsible for it."

Larry shook his head. "I understand. First let me get the tray to the table, then I'll be there for you."

Bob looked after their friend and couldn't hide a smile. In his tight pants and the silk shirt, Larry would fit perfectly into the world of actors and artists.

Larry sauntered back. "Okay, first of all, what can I bring you? I've created a new burger, low carb. You'll like it, Bob. And for you—" Larry beamed at Steve. "—I recommend a taco, filled with meat and onions, just spicy enough to take your breath away."

"That's it!" Steve rubbed his hands in anticipation.

"What're you guys up to?" Larry drew two beers for them.

"We've got an invitation to that new club, Steps to Heaven," Bob explained. "We strongly believe that's where Blue Rocket is coming from."

"Steps to Heaven?" Larry gazed at them, impressed. "How'd two cops like you get into that place? There's a waiting list months long to join. I'm green with envy." Larry turned and shouted an order through the open kitchen door. The cook nodded, flipping a couple of burgers on the grill.

"Larry, do you know who runs the club? We're going undercover, and some info would be helpful," Bob said.

"I only heard that the DJ is one of a kind, and the bartender has a say in who can go back into the private rooms," Larry explained, looking thoughtful.

"Did you hear of any drugs being sold there?" Steve asked.

Larry nodded. "Word on the street is that somebody is experimenting with a new kind of speed that makes you feel more powerful and energetic. But only members of the club can get the stuff." Larry raised his hands. "I wish I could help you, but so far I've had no luck joining Steps to Heaven. It's only for models and actors."

"We know that. Any more hints?" Bob asked.

Larry pinched his nose. "Rumor says there's activity in the private back rooms that the police aren't supposed to know about. Gambling or selling the drugs. Could be both." Larry smirked. "I've heard that people who prefer a certain lifestyle are welcome in that club." He raised an eyebrow.

"Bob is going as an up-and-coming model, and I'm taking my camera with me," Steve said seriously. "We'll fit right in."

Bob answered in the affirmative, slapping his partner on the back.

TWO HOURS later Bob lay in his bed, looking back on the last week. He was restless. He put his arm under the pillow and tried to find a comfortable position.

Why had Steve reacted so badly when Bob suggested they go undercover as a gay couple? What was his hang-up? Bob had never known Steve to be so skittish about playing a part. Especially one as easy as this one.

Jessica came to his mind.

Had Steve really been interested in that girl? Bob couldn't believe that was possible. She had just been a way into the club, a source of information. And once Steve had gotten over his hurt feelings, he'd been fine on the trip through Santa Barbara and Bakersfield.

No, it had to be something else bothering him. Possibly the juxtaposition of being groped by Randolph and having to play gay? Was Steve really that repulsed by two men together? Except that Steve had had no problem sleeping in the same bed at the hotel. In fact, Bob had felt something very close to arousal coming off him when they lay head to toe.

Was it possible? Hope welled up inside him. He wanted to believe that Steve was attracted to him. Did Steve feel the same way he did but was just afraid to speak the truth?

A KNOCK sounded on the door, and Bob hastily zipped his pants, adjusting his crotch in the tight space. "Coming," he shouted, buttoning his jade shirt and grabbing the black boots on his way to the door.

"Wow!" Steve stood in the entrance and gazed at his friend, openmouthed.

Steve took his time examining Bob from head to toe. Under that azure gaze, Bob felt very uncomfortable. He'd spent more than half an hour searching his closet for just the right outfit to wear to the club. Finally, after sweating and cursing, he had found the pants he had worn when he first went to a disco. That was years ago. The pants still fit, although they were somewhat tighter than when he'd originally bought them. Maybe he should change into another pair?

"Clear the deck for action! Scrumptious!" Steve reached up to fumble with Bob's shirt to straighten the collar.

"Hey, what're you up to?" Bob batted his hand away, feeling scrutinized.

"Unbutton some more buttons, pal. You look gorgeous," Steve said softly, almost tenderly. He smiled slightly as if he wasn't sure what he was seeing.

Bob stared at his friend. He had the feeling that Steve was looking at him with different eyes. He saw love and desire there, and then Steve averted his gaze, holding up his camera.

"I bought this camera with the money I earned from working as a taxi driver when I came to the West Coast." He held it up, peering through the viewfinder. "I just took a picture of my beautiful black lady."

Steve beamed, pointing out the window at the Thunderbird parked at the curb. The early twilight caused the car to look pitch-black.

Bob admitted they would certainly look the part of a model and his photographer driving up in Steve's car. His Mercedes was too old-fashioned. He shrugged and left his apartment.

Steve said, "Hey, don't forget to put your boots on. Or do you plan to carry them under your arm?"

Bob shook his head, realizing he still had his boots under his arm. "You're an ass, you know that?" he said, bending down to put them on. This was not his day, he thought, wincing. His pants really were too tight. *Too late to change now.*

"You should take your leather jacket. It could be chilly by the time we leave." Steve walked past Bob into the apartment, letting his hand linger for a moment on Bob's back.

The caress made Bob feel warm, protected, and safe. "The jacket is on the chair in the bedroom," Bob shouted after his friend.

"Here we go." Steve came out of the apartment and held up Bob's black leather jacket. "I haven't got my gun. Didn't want to risk it," Steve said.

"Good idea."

"It's time, partner. I don't want Jessica to wait for us too long." Steve handed Bob the jacket and swaggered to the car.

Bob watched his partner's ass all the way down the stairs. Steve wasn't wearing his old washed-out jeans. He must have bought new ones, which were just as tight as the old ones—maybe tighter. Bob took a steadying breath. He liked the view just fine, which was very confusing.

"You coming?" Steve went around the car to unlock the doors.

Bob made a face at Steve's nagging and walked stiffly to the passenger side. His tight slacks were riding up the crack in his butt. He longed for his comfortable corduroys, and the action hadn't even started yet.

Chapter Nine

THE BUILDING looked like any other warehouse on the outskirts of Culver City except for the sign over the closed front door. "Steps to Heaven" was written in big red illuminated letters on the wall. What was astonishing was that there were so many people waiting patiently for admittance.

"Damn! Can you tell me how to find a fuckin' parking place that isn't miles away from the club?" Steve ranted after he'd gone around the block for the third time. "Hey, the police are allowed to park in front of the main entrance when there's evidence of a crime," he said half jokingly just as a big limousine pulled out of a parking space.

"Take that one!" Bob pointed to an opening with a sigh of relief. His tight pants were so uncomfortable. Why the hell had he chosen them? Maybe to impress Steve? Scrambling out of the car, he told himself to keep his mind on the Blue Rocket investigation and not on what his partner might think about him.

Checking out what the men and women waiting in line were wearing, Bob was glad to see that he wasn't overdressed in his tight black pants and jade silk shirt.

"Bob, Jessica's over there! She's waving at us." Steve threaded through the crowd of partygoers lined up on the sidewalk by the entrance.

"Hi there!" Jessica greeted them and gave Steve a kiss on the cheek. "Steve, right? And your better half is—?"

"I'm Bob. Nice of you to wait for us." He joined the queue behind Jessica and looked around, watching the people. Most of them were young, the women wearing flashy clothes and a lot of makeup. Bob suspected some of the men were wearing makeup too.

"The line doesn't usually take too long, and besides, Bruno the bouncer knows me," Jessica said, fluffing her hair.

The line of hopeful patrons snaked down the street. A bouncer stood in front of the door with his hand on a velvet rope, letting in only the luckiest few in the queue. Bob watched as he let a young actor Bob had seen in a Coca-Cola ad and a pretty blonde girl into the inner sanctum.

"Bob, the door's open. We're next!" Impatiently Steve grabbed hold of Bob's sleeve, and they followed Jessica past the velvet rope and into the building. The door closed behind them.

The hall was dark, but hundreds of little sparkling lights suspended from the ceiling and outlining the doorframes showed the way. Bob felt like he was walking through a sky full of stars.

"Wow! Terrific, isn't it?" Steve whispered in his ear, still holding his sleeve.

"Yes, it is." Bob had to admit that the fairy lights in the darkness had a special effect on him. It was as if he had entered a different world where exciting things awaited. He had to keep reminding himself that they were on a case, and to think like a detective.

Jessica showed them into the main room, which had a bar and a large space for dancing. The place was huge and packed with people. More twinkling lights decorated every surface. There was no music. Obviously the party hadn't started yet.

"Boys, have fun, and enjoy yourselves. I'm meeting some other friends, but I'll be back later. See you." She flashed a smile in Steve's direction and was gone.

"Jessica…," Steve said forlornly.

"Get over her. You're supposed to be with me, remember?" Bob leaned over until his head touched Steve's, feeling the familiar texture of Steve's hair on his cheek.

Abruptly Steve drew away. "Bob, leave it, huh? It's enough that we're undercover, but stop giving the impression that you're my boyfriend." He nodded at the bar, lined with the beautiful people wanting to be seen by the rich and powerful.

"Make yourself at home, and try to find out who the boss is. I'll try my luck at the bar." Steve pushed through the mash of bodies, away from Bob.

Bob felt like he had been kicked in the gut. He couldn't believe Steve had accused him of acting too touchy-feely. Where was the guy who had checked him out so intimately at the door that night?

Bob shrugged. Steve had been running hot and cold all week. This wasn't something he could dwell on now. He was on an assignment and needed to check out the club. He wandered over to the bar but had to wait until a miniskirted waitress picked up a tray full of drinks before he could get a space. The bartender was busy making what Bob privately called "froufrou drinks"—brightly colored confections trimmed with umbrellas and fruit.

"Banana daiquiri," Bob ordered. He had to shout because the music had started, and half the barflies gravitated to the dance floor.

Donna Summer's "Last Dance" got the place jumping. As the last notes ended, DJ Ronnie welcomed the audience. "Hey, my babies!" Ronnie crooned into the microphone. "Welcome to Steps to Heaven!"

The audience roared with approval, some screaming out his name.

Bob looked up. Ronnie had a booth just above the north end of the room. There was a big picture window, outlined in tiny white lights. He could easily see Ronnie, a black floppy hat on his head, slapping another record on the turntable. "Whaddaya say we groove to a little Led Zeppelin? It's our theme song, 'Stairway to Heaven'!"

Bob winced at a burst of white noise from the amplifiers as the famous lyrics poured out. He hummed along, waiting for the bartender to bring his drink.

The Bee Gees followed Led Zeppelin with "Night Fever." Obviously it was an oldie night.

"Would you like to dance?" someone asked him.

Bob looked down at a tiny woman with long red hair. Her smile was contagious, and before he realized it, he was on the dance floor with her.

If only Steve could see me. Normally he refused to dance because he couldn't quite get his body to move to the beat. Tonight was different. The festive mood and the stars sparkling from the ceiling had a strange impact on Bob. Forgetting the troubles of everyday life, he let the music carry him away.

His dance partner shook her red curls until they stood straight out. Turning around, she let loose, dancing with grace and abandon. Bob watched the way her eyes caught the lights when she threw back her head and twirled. The song changed to a slow tempo to let the dancers move into each other's arms.

The girl looked up at Bob, and he put his arms around her, pulling her close. Her soft hair tickled his cheek, and made him sneeze. "*Achoo!*"

"Gesundheit! By the way, I'm Cindy. I haven't seen you here before. Are you in showbiz?" Cindy giggled, swaying to Linda Ronstadt's "Blue Bayou."

Bob had to think before he answered with a smile. "I used to model, and I'm trying to get back in the game. It's not so easy, though…. You have to know the right people. What about you? You look like an actress I saw in *General Hospital* on TV. Weren't you the cute nurse cheering up her patients?"

His compliment pleased Cindy. She snuggled up to him, moving to the slow rhythm of the music. "I wish!" She giggled again. "I'd like to have a career in the movies, but so far I'm still waiting for the right guy to introduce me to the big boss." Cindy spoke into Bob's ear, leaning her head against his shoulder.

Cherishing the body of a woman pressed against him, Bob danced her across the floor. When the music ended, they stayed close to each other, and Bob remembered what he wanted to ask her. "You were talking about the boss. I'd like to get to know some important people too. Are there any big producers—any movers and shakers here tonight?"

Cindy frowned. "That's the problem. Nobody knows who actually owns this club, but I've heard that if you're invited to one of the back rooms, you're on your way to being famous. What's your name, by the way?"

"I'm Bob." He stuck out a hand, and she shook it with a mischievous glint in her eye. "And I could use a drink. Care to join me?" Bob led her back to the bar where he had left his daiquiri.

Apparently they were out of luck. A pretty girl with long black hair was sipping Bob's drink, chatting up a man in skintight leather pants.

"Over there." Cindy pointed to the corner right next to the door. Two men wearing matching purple jumpsuits were just leaving the bar area. Sitting down, Cindy winked at the barkeeper. "Juan, a Tequila Sunrise, and for my friend…?"

"Sex on the Beach," Bob said, wondering why he had chosen that particular drink.

Cindy giggled. "I'd sure like to have sex on the beach with a guy like you." She waved a hand at the guys in purple dancing to "You're the One That I Want." "Most of the guys here are involved with another guy, if you get my drift.…"

Bob spotted Steve at the other end of the bar. He was head to head with a black man on his right. The broad-shouldered man was talking with his hands, making wide gestures to illustrate some point. He put his arm around Steve's shoulder, pulling him closer.

Forgetting Cindy, Bob watched his partner. He got the feeling that Steve wasn't happy being so close to his new friend, but he wasn't sure. Somehow Steve must have noticed him. For a moment their eyes locked, and Bob read in Steve's eyes *Glad you are here. Everything's okay.*

Bob gave Cindy a big smile even though he hadn't heard a word she'd said. He took a sip of his drink. Very sweet with hardly any taste of alcohol. "You said there are back rooms here?" He glanced around, but it was dark enough that he couldn't make out the doors to other rooms or back offices. "Shouldn't we try to find someone important to push our careers?"

"Let's ask Juan," Cindy said, waving at the harried barkeeper. "Juan, darling, is there any chance we could meet with some of the bigwigs? I saw some really influential people going into the back room." Cindy smiled prettily and batted her eyes. "I wanted a one-on-one with the boss for so long, and my new friend deserves to be seen. Isn't he a cutie?"

Bob felt himself blush at the praise.

Suspiciously Juan eyed Bob, and a smile lit his face. "I'll have a talk with the boss. In your case, Cindy, I have to disappoint you again. You should keep your job at the café. I told you at the last party that he isn't interested in your type. Maybe next year."

Cindy pouted, and Bob felt sorry for her. Looking at her in the brighter lights above the bar, he realized that she was older than he'd first thought. Obviously whoever was choosing had specific types in mind and didn't just take any new wannabe off the street.

"Hey." He leaned in closer to her, dropping his voice to a whisper. "Not our luckiest day, but I've heard that you can get stuff here to make you feel better. Have you ever tried Blue Rocket? Maybe it would cheer us up."

Cindy looked up at him, confused. "I always thought Blue Rocket was the movie they were planning to do. And they *are* looking for actors and models." She sighed. "I wanted to be chosen but never got further than the disco. You heard it. I'm not their type." She shook her head in disbelief. "You think Blue Rocket is a drug, and you're looking for it? Are you a user?" She put some distance between them.

Bob patted her arm to calm her. "No, but several models I know who frequent this club used Blue Rocket. A couple of them died. I just wanted to know if they got the stuff here."

"Sorry, I had no idea." Cindy picked up her Tequila Sunrise and took a sip, watching Juan mixing a drink in the blender.

Bob lowered his voice even more. "There was a well-known photographer, Randolph Foreman. He was found dead last week, murdered. Have you heard of him?"

Appalled, Cindy put her drink on the counter. "Once I met a photographer, and I think his name was Ray."

"Where did you meet him? Can you tell me more about him?" Bob smiled at her, hoping she could give him something more.

"Could have been here, but it wasn't at a party. When they opened the club, there was a reception and everything was free. You could have your photo taken by some of the top names, and one photographer was called Ray."

"Was he alone?" Bob asked.

"Really, I don't remember. There were so many people. I only remember asking him to take photos of me and how much it would cost. He said I should make an appointment with Fashion Photos where he worked. That's all."

"Another drink?" Juan interrupted their conversation.

"Just a moment," Bob replied. He had to talk to Steve and decide what to do next. Cindy wasn't much help, but maybe Juan had influence with the boss man and could get them in. Bob looked over to the other end of the bar and frowned. Steve and his new friend were gone. Searching through the horde of people in the club, Bob spotted his partner on the dance floor.

The guy from the bar had his arms around Steve, and they were slow dancing. Bob's heartbeat raced. He hated seeing the other man touching Steve that way. He couldn't imagine Steve agreeing to such an intimate dance after his vehemence about appearing gay in public.

At that moment the man ran his hand down Steve's back, coming to a halt on Steve's ass. Bob felt a rage he hadn't experienced before. He needed to know Steve was okay.

Steve and the black man danced nearer to the bar, and Bob finally caught Steve's eye. Steve didn't look comfortable at all.

Bob's belly clenched. Striding onto the dance floor, he tapped the man on the shoulder, interrupting the dance.

Before he could say anything, Steve said, "Hey, Bob!" He pulled away from the black man, patting Bob's belly at the same time. "Mike, this is my boyfriend. Sorry to dance and run." Steve put an arm around Bob's waist, leaning his head in the crook of Bob's neck.

Bob could feel Steve's relief but shook a finger at him to keep up appearances. "Where have you been, you naughty boy? I've looked for you everywhere." Bob gave him a reproachful glance before he leaned forward to kiss Steve on the cheek. He expected Steve to pull away and was surprised when Steve returned the kiss, lightly brushing his lips.

A jolt shot through Bob. He barely heard Mike say "Sorry, man, I didn't know… I understand" before retreating.

Bob took a deep breath. Steve was so close, and his body heat was seeping right into Bob's skin. He needed some space to recover from the kiss. He could still feel Steve's lips touching his. Backing up, he held Steve at arm's length. "Everything okay?"

Steve nodded, rolling his eyes. "Where'd you get to?"

"I met a girl, Cindy," Bob said. The music had started again, and it was so loud, he could feel it in the soles of his feet. "She doesn't know anything about Blue Rocket, but it's possible she met Randolph once."

Steve raised one eyebrow. "That's a...." A loud guitar riff from "Bohemian Rhapsody" cut off the end of Steve's sentence.

"What?" Bob yelled.

"That's a beginning!" Steve repeated.

"And what have you found out?" Bob asked, squeezing past gyrating men and women to get to the bar. He stepped on some guy's shoe, but the man didn't seem to notice, he was too busy smiling dreamily at a *Vogue* model.

"Apart from Mike's dancing abilities, not so much," Steve shouted in Bob's ear.

Bob turned around to hear him better. A couple of dancers boogied too near and almost pushed them apart.

Steve pulled Bob off the dance floor. "I asked Mike if he had ever tried Blue Rocket, and he admitted it had been an extraordinary experience. He felt dull and disoriented at first, but then he felt powerful, like he could succeed in whatever he wanted to do." Steve hooked an arm around Bob to talk directly into his ear. "Mike confided that he'd gotten pills in a back room, here in the club. But he doesn't know any names." Steve looked disappointed.

"At least we know you can get Blue Rocket in this club," Bob stated, very happy to have Steve's arm around him, even if it was just so they could talk.

"And Mike said that he tried Blue Rocket in pill form and it had a powerful effect on him. He had heard of people injecting the stuff, and they had some kind of nightmares. So he stayed with the pills." Steve sighed, inching over to the bar. Two women winked at him, sashaying off with their drinks.

"That's interesting." Bob nodded, spotting the cute redhead again. She raised an arm with a big smile. "Look, that's Cindy over there at the bar waving at us. She told me the boss, whoever he is, picks certain people and invites them into a private room. The chosen few get a chance to start a big career."

"And get the new drug there," Steve added. "We have to find out who the boss is."

"Juan, the bartender, already told me he'd mention me to the boss," Bob said, turning to the bar.

"Wow, your looks are at least good for something." Steve grinned and joined Bob at the bar. Touching Bob's arm or leaning against him, Steve made a big show of who he belonged with.

Bob smiled inwardly. It was nice to feel needed by his partner.

Cindy smiled ruefully. "Hi, Bob. I see I never had a real shot with you. That's the way it is around here. I was just about to leave." She shrugged philosophically. "Nothing to gain for me tonight."

"Cindy, this is my friend Steve," Bob introduced. "Could you ask Juan to put in a good word for him as well? Steve needs a job desperately." Bob smiled proudly at his partner, pretending to be besotted, which didn't take much pretending. "He's the best photographer I know."

Cindy looked at Steve doubtfully. Finally she shrugged. "I can try it again." Raising her hand, she called out, "Juan? Another Tequila Sunrise for me."

Juan waved a hand to indicate he'd be right over and placed four wineglasses on a waitress's tray. He dispensed beer and shots of whiskey to several people at the bar before pouring a shot of the drink for Cindy.

"Another Tequila Sunrise for the lady," Juan said graciously, sliding over a filled tumbler. Bob paid for her drink.

"Thank you!" Then Cindy addressed Juan. "I know what you said earlier." She smiled winningly. "And I've accepted my fate, but Steve here is a friend of Bob's. He's waiting for his chance. Can you do something for him?"

"Cindy, I've got a lot to do. As I told you...." Wiping the counter, Juan looked Steve and Bob up and down, and a little smile crossed his face. "I'll try what I can. Wait a sec." He retreated to a phone on the wall near the kitchen door.

Bob glanced at Steve. There was the unspoken question, *Will we get a chance to meet the owner?*

"Maybe, baby," Steve mumbled.

"I wish." Bob sighed, smiling at Cindy, who sipped her drink.

"Yes, ditto." She made a face, her disappointment obvious.

After a short while, Juan came back, smiling apologetically. "Sorry, guys. There's no activity in the back room tonight. Maybe next time." He collected a few empty glasses off the bar and stashed them in the sink. "You just have to keep coming back. Only a lucky few get the big break." He waved a hand at customers down the bar and poured out three beers. "We just finished casting for the fashion movie *Ice Fever*. You might have read about it. It's going to be a great success." He turned away to hand the beers to three young poseurs and flirted with a sweet girl at the same time.

"Juan, one more question." Bob leaned on the counter, waving to get the bartender's attention again.

"I wonder who he has just talked to on the phone," Steve mumbled, watching the bartender approach.

"Whaddaya want?" Juan wiped a glass clean before pouring a pink concoction out of his blender.

"I've heard about some good stuff available here," Bob said, pretending to toss back a few pills.

Juan leaned in very close and hissed, "Dunno what you mean. And now excuse me, I have a job to do." He turned away, looking annoyed.

"This is a bust," Steve said, smacking the bar.

Bob raised his eyebrows. They really needed to find out about the owners, as well as anyone else who worked behind the scenes at Steps to Heaven.

Cindy tugged on Steve's sleeve. "Steve, maybe I can help you," she whispered.

With the ambient noise level, it was almost impossible to hear her, but Bob went with her when she motioned for him and Steve to follow her. In a dark corner, near the door to the restrooms, she stopped. "I've often noticed that people go back that way." She pointed to a hall that led to a staircase. "This scene hasn't worked out for me. I'm leaving. See you again?" She looked at Bob longingly.

He bent down to kiss her on the cheek. "Who knows, Cindy? It was nice to meet you," Bob said, watching as she melted into the crowd of merrymakers on the dance floor.

DJ Ronnie suddenly announced, "Another song by one of the best groups of 1978—"How Deep is your Love" by the Bee Gees!"

Barry Gibb's falsetto harmonies poured out of the loudspeakers.

"What're we gonna do now?" Steve looked at his watch. The illuminated face showed 11:00 p.m.

"Juan said nothing was going on in the back rooms, whatever that means." Bob peered up the stairwell. "Let's take a peek anyway, what do you think?"

"Could be worth it," Steve said. "Maybe we'll find evidence of secret drug meetings, dealers, high customers...." Steve didn't sound very hopeful, though.

"And meet the boss." Bob smirked. "Come on, let's check the basement first." He turned to the dark hall.

"Just a sec." Steve motioned to the nearby restrooms. "Be right back."

"Yeah. Okay."

Near the staircase, he saw a phone on the wall. Bob thought about calling Rollins to tell him about the club, when one of the doors at the end of the hall opened and a man stepped out. Bob only saw the silhouette of a broad-chested guy. Something in his appearance was familiar, but Bob couldn't figure out why.

The huge man disappeared into another room, leaving the door ajar. Bob crept closer, hoping to listen in on whatever the man was doing. He stayed against the wall, well hidden in the darkness, and put his ear against the door.

With a sudden movement, the door swung open and hit Bob on the head. Pain shot through his ear and he jerked back, suppressing a yelp.

"What do we have here?" Rough hands pulled him up and dragged him into the room.

Bob groaned, feeling dizzy and out of control.

Chapter Ten

STEVE CAME out of the restroom, refreshed. *Where the heck has Bob gone?* Steve scanned the gyrating crowd, trying to locate him.

Swaying to the music, Steve frowned as he took a quick walk around the club. Bob was nowhere in sight. Not on the dance floor, not at the bar or sitting at any of the small tables clustered on the far side of the room.

"Hey, where are you?" Steve mumbled. "You weren't supposed to go off on your own."

Alarmed, he headed to the back hall where the restrooms were located, but he couldn't see Bob.

"Shit!" Steve had a queasy feeling in his stomach, a foreboding that Bob was in trouble. He decided to call the station.

The desk sergeant had just answered when someone yanked the receiver out of his hand and snarled, "Pig!"

Something round and hard pushed into his side, and Steve knew he was in trouble.

"Hey, man, what's up?" Steve said, going for cool. "I'm looking for my boyfriend." He tried to twist away from the pistol in his ribs, but the attacker shoved him away from the telephone and against the wall. He started to speak as he looked into the bartender's cold eyes. "What the f—"

"Shut up!" Juan said, swinging his arm.

A sudden pain shot through Steve's skull as something cold and metallic hit him on the back of the head.

Dazed, Steve kicked out with one leg and connected to something, but he was too disoriented to fight effectively. Juan grabbed him and roughly propelled him into a room. Steve stumbled and almost fell, but Juan caught him under the armpits, cursing.

The bright overhead light hurt Steve's eyes and he squeezed them shut trying not to vomit. His arms were yanked behind him and tied securely together. He stood on wobbly legs. From the opposite corner of the room, he heard a man's forced laughter.

"When it rains, it pours!" a deep voice said. "Why are two cops nosing around my establishment? I'm waiting for an answer, Detective!"

Steve had heard that voice somewhere, but with the pain in his head, he couldn't quite place it.

"I know you," Steve mumbled. He looked into the face of John Sanders. "Sanders? You run this club?"

"I'm waiting!" snarled Sanders. With an impatient grunt, he gave Juan a sign.

Juan slugged Steve hard in the belly, sending him to his knees. Steve gagged, barely able to breathe, and toppled onto his side.

"What were you looking for?" Sanders stepped down on Steve's side and pressed hard.

"My boyfriend," Steve whimpered, choking back the bile in his throat.

"You mean this guy?" Sanders gave him a last kick for good measure and walked over to a big armchair. He turned it around with a flourish.

"Bob!" Steve gasped, curling into his aching belly.

Bob hunched limply in the chair, staring absently into space. He showed no reaction when Steve called his name.

Sanders lifted one of Bob's eyelids and frowned. "Chris better not have overdosed him!" he groused. "We've got to get him to walk a long way, right?"

"Sure, Boss," Juan said quickly. He stood guard over Steve with his pistol in hand.

"What the hell did you give him?" Steve finally got a decent breath, which helped clear his head. He climbed slowly to his knees, marshaling all his waning strength.

Sanders laughed without humor. "You know very well. Randolph was about to tell you all about our little business." Sanders exchanged glances with Juan and inclined his head.

Juan yanked Steve to his feet. Sweating, Steve leaned against the wall, fighting nausea.

"What does Randolph have to do with your business here?" Steve hissed. "Why don't you fill me in? First, tell me what you gave my friend."

Bob moaned and looked around. Steve tried to get Bob's attention, hoping to see the familiar sparkle in those eyes, but he only saw confusion.

The door opened, and Chris Barber stepped in. Steve gaped in surprise.

"Is the van ready?" Sanders asked.

Chris nodded.

"Chris? What are you doing here?" Steve moved his hands to loosen the rope around them to try to get free. It was a nightmare, seeing Sanders and Chris in front of him.

"None of your business!" Chris said curtly, grabbing Bob's arm. He and Sanders hauled the limp Bob out of the chair.

Steve couldn't bear the sight of Bob looking so weak. "What did you drug him with? Leave him alone!" he cried, kicking at Juan, who stepped nimbly out of the way. Steve sagged in defeat.

What if they had given Bob Blue Rocket? Mike said his first reaction to the drug left him feeling dull and unfocused, and Bob looked like that. "I have to know what…." Steve tried to get up.

"We'll take care of you two lovebirds, don't worry," Sanders spat. "Juan, push Steve out the door."

Manhandled into the dark hall, Steve started to shout for help, but the pistol Chris pointed at Bob's head stilled his voice. He could hear the pulsing beat from the disco music on the dance floor. The DJ's humorous comments sounded as if they came from another world.

Sanders and Chris dragged Bob to the back exit. Juan shoved Steve in front of him. Cool night air hit Steve in the face, and he inhaled deeply. Whatever they planned to do, he had to be ready to fight his way out and get Bob to safety.

There was a black van in the alley behind the club. Chris hauled Bob over to it, shifting him to one side to open the door. Bob lolled, his limbs hanging loosely. He put up no resistance when Chris and Sanders managed to get him inside.

"Move!"

Roughly, Juan shoved Steve into the back of the van. Steve ended up lying on Bob's lap. Bob groaned, moving sluggishly. Steve shifted carefully to give him more room. Had Bob been given the Blue Rocket drug?

"Pal, I'm right here. Don't worry." Steve's hands were still tied. He yearned to touch his partner, to reassure him that he wasn't alone. Instead he leaned his head against Bob's chest and felt his steady heartbeat through the sweat-soaked shirt. Frantically, Steve tried to come up with a way to escape, but Bob was as weak as a kitten. There was no way Steve would leave Bob alone.

Sanders and Chris took a seat in front. Craning his head, Steve saw there was a third man, sitting behind the wheel. His broad shoulders filled half of the front row. Sanders and Chris sat cramped in their seats.

"What are you waiting for, Freddie? Go!" Sanders ordered, looking back at Steve and Bob. "What a sight! Too bad I don't have my camera with me. The lovebirds, united for all eternity. Freddie, you know what to do when we arrive?"

"Sure, Boss. Randall and Curry busted me two years ago, and it'll be a pleasure to blow these cops away," Freddie boasted. He laughed— a sound that made Steve's blood freeze.

Steve held his breath. He knew that laughter. It was Freddie, Bella's husband. Freddie, the man who had sold drugs on schoolyards before they arrested him and put him behind bars. Steve recalled talking to many of the schoolkids, who all mentioned the drug dealer's hearty laughter. He had seemed so kind and gained their trust easily by handing out free samples. With that, he had them hooked.

Steve hated him.

"Bob? Come on, wake up, I need you," Steve whispered.

Sanders turned around at the sound. "That's it, pigs," he said coldly. "I've got a great idea of how to get rid of two problems at once."

Freddie laughed again, his broad shoulders moving up and down. "Boss, you're incredible. It'll be an honor to show you I deserve your respect."

"Freddie Garner!" Steve raised his voice. "Why are you out of jail already? And what about your wife?"

The big man turned around, a triumphant smile on his face. "Detective, sometimes you have to take your chances, combine your old life with a new one. I did that right!"

"Think of Bella!" Steve insisted.

Freddie snorted. "None of your business, pig!" He looked at Sanders. "The place we talked about earlier, Boss?"

"Exactly. Turn left at the next intersection. A wonderful place to make love—and die."

Chris giggled. He raised a pistol, pretending to shoot. "I'm ready for action!"

"Put it back!" Sanders barked.

Chris fell silent. Reluctantly he shoved the weapon into the shelf between the seats.

Bob must have felt Steve's agitation. Sluggishly, he sat up straighter. "Mmm, where am I? Steve?" He patted Steve's head and sighed, sounding content. "Good to be with you, pal."

"Not so good. Look who's there, planning to get rid of us," Steve said, shifting his wrists back and forth to loosen the tight rope. He was tied too securely. All his twisting had rubbed the skin raw, and he could feel blood on his wrists. He moaned in frustration.

"Soon your troubles will be over." A malicious smile played across Sanders's lips. Steve saw it in the rearview mirror. His worries increased. *What have we gotten into?*

"I know him," Bob mumbled, looking more alert.

"Yeah," Steve whispered near Bob's ear. "It's Randolph's boss, Sanders. Don't make a fuss, but can you get my hands free? They're tied." He wiggled around so that Bob could have access to his bindings.

He felt Bob's fingers skittering against the ropes, but Bob was still too drugged to make sense of the knots.

Steve felt the van move up into the hills.

"There's the entrance to North Park," Freddie said.

Bob tugged at the ropes around Steve's wrists again. Steve grinned. "Good boy," he said quietly.

Bob snorted softly, untying one of the knots.

"Shut up, you in the back!" snarled Sanders. He sounded nervous all of a sudden.

"Shut up, you!" Steve countered. "I'll bet you murdered Randolph, didn't you?"

"Freddie, round the next corner," Sanders ordered, ignoring Steve's comment. He sounded determined. "You know what to do. That blond cop killed Randolph, out of jealousy. His cop lover here is next. You got it?" Sanders took his pistol and wrapped a cloth around it….

"What about me? What's my part in the game?" Chris asked.

"Later, later." Sanders seemed to be on edge.

"Just a moment, Boss. Have to park." Freddie stopped the van and waited for more orders.

Steve swore silently under his breath. *Well, at least we know the plan now.* And if Bob's wits were returning, they just might have a chance to get away. "C'mon!" he hissed at Bob.

Bob's fingernails dug into Steve's wrists, but Steve didn't care as long as he was untied.

"Yeah, the blond cop shot his partner's lover. And then he shoots his partner for going behind his back with another guy." Freddie sounded like he was trying to convince himself that this would work.

"Better walk 'em down into the ravine," Chris suggested. "This place is really overgrown. Nobody'll see their bodies for weeks."

"First I kill Randall, then I turn the gun on Curry so it'll look like he killed himself," Freddie continued nervously. "Great plan, boss!"

"Don't blow it, Garner!" Sanders warned. "I'll watch what you do. It's your ticket to the executive suite, so give me proof that I can trust you."

Sanders handed the weapon to Freddie. "Keep this cloth around it until you put it into the dead cop's hand."

Freddie held the gun with a proud expression on his face.

Steve was near puking. *What an ass! I'm going to throw Freddie back in the slammer if it's the last thing I do. Bella really has bad taste in husbands.*

Freddie climbed out of the van, pacing around the vehicle, talking to himself. Mumbling something Steve couldn't hear, Chris opened the van door and followed Freddie.

Bob tried to sit up straighter. "We have to get out of here." He grabbed Steve's arm in a fierce grip.

"Sure, buddy. Everything's going to be all right." Steve leaned over, and they touched foreheads. Watching their captors out of the corner of his eye, Steve rubbed his wrists together, using the blood as a lubricant to slip the ropes off.

"Shh," Bob whispered, still working on the tightest knot.

"What's that idiot doing?" Chris asked, tapping on the glass from the outside. "Get out of the car, cops, pronto!"

Freddie popped his head back into the open driver's door. "Listen, Boss, my wife knows these guys. I don't know about this."

"We agreed, Freddie," Sanders said blandly. "This is your initiation. If you want to move up the ladder, you have to take out the trash."

"Nobody will believe that Bob murdered Randolph!" Steve yelled angrily. "We were together that night."

"Yeah, y'know...," Freddie started.

Sanders smiled. "But who cares when they're dead?"

He climbed out of the van, and Steve heard them all walking around to the back.

Steve's bonds were looser and hung around his wrists. He held onto the frayed ends of the rope to make it look like they were tighter than they really were.

When the back doors opened up, Chris and Freddie grabbed Steve and Bob, hauling them out. Steve struggled and managed to kick Chris in the shin. Bob was still unsteady, but even in the dark, Steve saw determination in his face. They would get through this together. Bob leaned weakly on Steve when they were on their feet.

Sanders said, "Freddie, you know the way. Along the path, and then there's a quiet place on the right. The perfect spot for two fags to make love, hate, and kill each other."

"What about fingerprints?" Freddie asked, sounding nervous.

"Dummy, I wiped the gun clean. Just put the gun in Curry's hand after you kill him, then there will be only the cop's prints on the weapon," Sanders snapped. "Just don't be dumb enough to touch the pistol yourself." Sanders pointed to the path. "Hurry. And before you leave the bodies, check to see they're dead. I'll be watching you."

"Should I check on the job too?" Chris asked, moving down the path. He shined a flashlight into the inky dark trees, illuminating a path.

"When it's done, yes. Stay with me now. I don't like the dark," Sanders said.

Planning to fight his way out and make a run for it, Steve wasn't sure if Sanders was joking or not.

"Get ready," Steve said sotto voce into Bob's ear. Bob nodded, his hair tickling Steve's mouth.

Standing slightly behind Bob to shield his movements, Steve wrenched the rope from his wrists. He peered at his watch. Grateful for the illuminated dial, he pushed down on the button, twisting it carefully to select the function he needed. Then he unfastened it and threw it across the road.

"Attention, attention!" The sound coming from the watch was astoundingly loud.

Sanders whirled around. "What the hell was that?" he yelled. "Chris, were we followed?"

"No!" Chris flashed the light into the bushes.

Freddie took a few steps forward. "You think it's the police?" he asked anxiously.

When the three men had their backs to Steve and Bob, Steve grabbed Bob's arm. "Move, buddy," he whispered. He and Bob dove into the underbrush. Bob was still unsteady, and Steve had to drag him behind the next bush.

Lying flat on his stomach, Steve didn't dare breathe. He kept one hand on Bob's back, to assure himself he was still there.

"Freddie, go after them!" Sanders yelled. "It was some kind of trick!"

"They went over there!" Freddie ran far too close to the bush where Steve and Bob lay.

Steve longed for his gun and winced when the flashlight found them.

"How cute! Look, they want to make love for the last time!" Chris kicked Bob with his boot. "Get up! Quicker!"

Bob groaned and tried to roll away. Chris gave him another kick.

"Fuck off!" Steve yelled.

Bob kicked out with both legs, but he missed Barber and only hit air. Chris hauled him upright, laughing.

"Leave it, buddy," Steve soothed, climbing to his knees. "There must be another way to get outta here."

Bob went limp in Chris's grip, but Steve could see that he was seething with anger.

"I can't wait to put an end to this," Freddie growled.

"Then what are you waiting for?" Sanders nodded. "We've been here far too long."

Freddie shoved the gun into Steve's ribs, forcing him and Bob along the dirt path. Stumbling along in the inky woods, Steve could hear Freddie's heavy breathing behind them. Frantically he thought of another way to escape.

"Hey…." Bob whispered.

"What is it?" Steve said. Only a little tremble in his voice betrayed his fear.

"I heard something. Didn't you hear that?" Bob said, stumbling forward.

"Your partner is clever," Freddie said softly, his voice barely audible. He moved closer so they stood bunched together under a eucalyptus tree. "Guys, I'm on your side. Play along with me. You go over there." He pushed his weapon into Bob's back.

"Freddie, what…?" Steve gasped. He didn't know what to say.

"I'm working undercover for Vice. Trust me."

Steve turned and peered at Freddie. The man grinned, his teeth white in the dark night. "Back to business," he said more seriously. "Curry shoots you, and after that, he kills himself." Freddie motioned Steve to sit opposite Bob on the cold ground.

"But…." Steve protested, trying to figure out what was going on.

"Trust him," Bob said, making no effort to touch the pistol.

Freddie crouched beside him. "I put the weapon in your hand, and I force you to pull the trigger."

"And I have to pretend to shoot my partner." Bob sounded much more alert. He took the pistol carefully, pointing it at the ground.

"You were never a very good shot," Steve joked, but his throat was tight. They still weren't out of the woods.

"We have to hurry before that weasel Chris comes to check on the dead meat." Freddie gave Bob a sign.

"Bob, what are you doing?" Steve raised his voice loudly enough for Sanders and Barber to hear. "Honey, what about all we mean to each other?"

"This is for Randolph!" Bob shouted, putting hatred into his words. He pulled the trigger. The bullet whizzed past Steve and hit the next tree.

"Good," Freddie said quietly. "Steve, you're hit!"

Steve sank to the ground, slumping against the tree.

"Impressive, Camille," Bob said, referring to the novel they'd studied at school. Normally, it was a joke between them, but now his voice was tense.

They heard steps approaching. Steve closed his eyes to slits, watching the drama in front of him.

Freddie turned into the cold and aggressive drug dealer he was supposed to be. He held the weapon alongside Bob's head and pulled the trigger.

"That's it, pig!" he shouted. Then he whispered, "You're dead. Act that way." And he was gone, melting into the dark night.

From the distance Steve and Bob heard Chris shout, "Man, that took an eternity! Let me check on it, Boss!"

Steve held his breath and heard Freddie speak out loud, "The pig cops are as dead as they can be. Got it?"

"Hurry up, Garner," Sanders said urgently. "We have a job to do."

"We're coming," Freddie said, dragging Chris with him through the underbrush back to the clearing where the van waited. "It was simply a pleasure seeing my worst enemies die. They're dead as a doornail." Freddie laughed hysterically, and Chris joined in.

Chapter Eleven

BOB LAY on his side, not moving, his ears still throbbing from the gun blast so close to his head. He prayed that Chris Barber or Sanders wouldn't come back to check on them. The rocky ground poked his back, but he didn't mind. The pain was the best sensation he had had in years.

I'm alive!

We're alive!

He wondered how Steve felt, but he didn't dare raise his head. He heard the engine of a car in the distance and possibly footsteps. He held his breath, pretending to be dead.

Then there was only silence. He breathed in shallow breaths, afraid that Sanders, Barber, or Freddie would come back, seeking proof that he and Steve were dead. He didn't know how much time went by, but after a while, he risked peering around. The van had disappeared, and nobody was in sight.

Bob looked around for Steve—and froze. Steve wasn't there! Bob raised his head and braced on an elbow, his heartbeat racing. Had they taken Steve without him noticing? He breathed out in relief when he heard a familiar voice behind him.

"Thank God, we're alive!"

"Steve! Where have you been?" Bob looked around worriedly, making sure they were alone in the woods.

Steve crouched beside him. "Couldn't wait. Had to take a leak. The coast is clear." Steve stood and reached out a hand to help him up.

Bob shuddered, feeling cold and wobbly.

"What did they do to you? You look awful!" Steve put his arm around Bob's shoulder and pulled him close.

For a moment Bob let go and leaned into Steve, savoring the warmth of his friend's body. He straightened, finger combing his disheveled hair. "I was such an idiot in the club. I was eavesdropping, trying to hear the conversation in the office," Bob said. "Suddenly the door opened and hit my head." He checked his skull, feeling a lump there.

"Didn't I tell you to wait for me?" Steve stroked Bob's back, pulling some pine needles out of Bob's silky shirt in the process.

"Yeah, I just wanted to take a look because I saw a guy who looked familiar. He disappeared into that room at the end of the hall." Bob sighed.

"That was Freddie Garner. Come on. We have to find help and get you checked into a hospital." Steve took Bob's arm to lead him back to the road.

"Wait! The pistol! We need it for evidence!" Bob hunched over, searching the shadowy ground for the gun. He got down on his hands and knees, feeling around under the brush. He touched the barrel before he saw it poking out from under a clump of blackberry bushes. "There it is!"

"They'll find your fingerprints on it," Steve said and picked the weapon up, making sure to keep the cloth Freddie had discarded wrapped securely around it.

"Did they really think the police would believe this story?" Bob fumed. "That I killed Randolph and murdered you out of jealousy? Then committed suicide?" Bob snorted, walking up the slope of the ravine. He swayed slightly and had to grab Steve's arm.

"They drugged you, Bob. We have to go to the hospital!" Steve said urgently, supporting him.

"Hospital? No way! They injected me with something that made me dizzy, Steve. I don't have Blue Rocket in my system."

"How do you know that?"

Bob felt Steve's strong arms tighten around his waist to help him walk more steadily. He stopped abruptly. "What if they come back and see us on the roadside?"

"We have to take that risk. I think they're more worried about cleaning up wherever they have the drug lab," Steve mused, checking the road in both directions. They walked downhill for a short distance, moving slowly because it was very dark, and Steve didn't want to trip over something he couldn't see.

He nearly ran into a signpost and peered up at the words: "Scenic viewpoint. Turnaround area 500 feet."

"Maybe we'll get lucky," Bob said softly.

"Look, Bob!" Steve poked him in the ribs, pointing down to the turnaround. "Do you see that parked car over there? It's hidden under the trees. A couple of lovebirds spending the night together, I'll bet."

"Our chance to get away," Bob said. Supported by Steve, he slowly crossed the road.

Steve knocked on the passenger-side window.

HALF AN hour later, they arrived at the precinct.

"Sara, Joey, we can't thank you enough for the ride!" Bob said sincerely, climbing out of the Mustang's cramped backseat.

"Yeah, we would've been stranded up there for hours!" Steve said. He pulled out a fifty from his back pocket. "For the inconvenience. It's dangerous to park so far out of town."

"We hear you!" Joey grinned, grabbing the money.

"Stay safe!" Sara called, waving as Joey pulled the red Mustang out of Steve's usual parking place in front of the building.

Steve and Bob mounted the front steps and entered the building.

"I'll call Rollins," Bob said wearily. "We need to brief him."

"I'll get rid of this thing." Steve took the gun down to Evidence and logged it in. This was an important link in the chain of evidence, even if the only fingerprints were Bob's. He was still reeling from their near miss. They would be dead if it hadn't been for Freddie. Where was he?

"Where's the night shift?" Steve complained and walked up to the abandoned squad room.

"Rollins's on his way in, I'll put out an APB on Sanders and Barber," Bob said, and dialed the number for Dispatch. "Hope I get someone there, at least." Bob checked the clock on the wall. "It's past midnight."

Steve looked at his wrist. "My watch!" His arms were bloody and raw from the tight rope, and his watch was gone.

"You sacrificed the watch for a noble cause," Bob said. "We got away. That alarm did the trick. I didn't even know it could speak English."

"We also should inform Vice about Freddie. I hope he's not in any danger," Steve said, picking up the coffeepot for something drinkable.

"He saved our lives," Bob stated dryly.

"Here you are." Steve offered him a cup of hot coffee and sat on the edge of Bob's desk.

"What a night! Now we know that John Sanders and Chris Barber are responsible for what's going on in the club," Bob said, sipping the hot liquid.

"And they tried to kill us!" Steve exclaimed.

They heard heavy footsteps, and Rollins burst into the office. He looked at the detectives. "You look rough. Come into my office." He opened the door, walked around his desk, and sat down with a sigh. "Take a seat."

Steve and Bob slumped down in the two armchairs in front of Rollins's desk.

"Fill me in on what happened tonight." Rollins pulled a small pillbox out of his jacket pocket. "The way you two are running around like lunatics does nothing for my stomach. Steve, get me some water, please."

Steve got up and filled a small cup from the cooler. "Sir, did you know that Freddie Garner was working undercover with Vice to infiltrate Sanders's gang?"

"This is the first I've heard of it," Rollins said grimly.

"He deserves a medal. He saved our skin," Bob explained, rubbing his temple. "We'd never have made it out of there without his help. We need to get Vice in on this."

"Bob and I went undercover to Steps to Heaven, ready for the big time," Steve said, perching on the arm of Bob's chair. "Our contact, Jessica, didn't know much, but we got some information that something has been going on in the private back rooms, maybe gambling and selling drugs."

"Were you able to get evidence of that?" Rollins asked, leaning forward.

"When I tried to investigate, Freddie, acting on Sanders's orders, overpowered me," Bob said.

"Sanders and Barber drugged Bob, but I don't think they used Blue Rocket," Steve said with concern.

Bob waved it off. "It was only something to make me dizzy and helpless, nothing serious."

"Have you been to a doctor yet? You have to be looked over." Worry lines appeared on Rollin's forehead.

"Maybe later. I'm fine," Bob assured his superior.

"What about the gun you turned in to ballistics?" Rollins asked, taking notes, all grumpiness gone.

"I bet it's the gun Randolph was killed with." Steve took a long breath. "Sanders wanted Freddie Garner to kill me and make it look like Bob did it. He was supposed to kill himself afterward. Only Garner managed to tell us that he was undercover and faked our deaths."

"We think one of them killed Randolph Foreman," Bob said. "And they wanted to make it look like Steve and I were jealous of each other, and I killed him for being with Randolph."

"Thank God you're alive." Rollins relaxed visibly.

"I spoke to a guy who took Blue Rocket. Customers could get it in the back rooms, that's for sure," Steve said, wincing when he flexed his sore wrist to pick up his coffee cup.

"Did you see any people who were obviously high? How do they take it?" Rollins wanted to know.

Steve thought for a moment. "Mike said he took a pill and felt the effect of the drug pretty quickly."

"Lieutenant, we should raid the place right away," Bob said grimly.

Rollins looked at the clock on his desk. "I'm trying to send a team over to the club." He grabbed the phone to make the call.

"Nothing better than that!" Steve got up.

"Sit down, Steve!" Rollins said with determination. "You had a long day, which ended with an assault. I want you out of danger." Rollins crossed his arms. "Bob, take your partner home. You both need some shut-eye." Calling them by their first names showed his concern for the detectives.

"But we've been to the club. We know where to look…." Bob protested.

"Look at yourself. You both look terrible. Go home. That's an order!" Rollins barked and pointed to the door.

All of a sudden, Steve acknowledged his fatigue. He held the door open for Bob. His partner looked as exhausted as he did. Rollins was right, they'd be no use in the raid.

Before leaving the room, Bob turned around. "In the morning we'll be in early to find out what they found at Steps to Heaven. I wonder if Sanders and Barber went back to the club."

"One more reason to stay in the background," Rollins said. "You don't want to let them know you're still alive and that Freddie Garner didn't do his job properly."

"Boss, you're right." Steve nodded, suppressing a yawn.

"We put out the APB, and warrants are in place to arrest Sanders and Barber," Bob said wearily, sipping the last of his cooling coffee.

"I wish you'd gone to the doctor so we could find out what they gave you," Steve grumbled. "I'm beat, let's get out of here."

"To MY place?" Bob asked as they sat in his old Mercedes.

"Wherever you want to go," Steve agreed. He was concerned. "Are you up to driving? How are you feeling?"

"A bit cold, and I feel lousy in these tight pants and boots," Bob said, relaxing when Steve gently rubbed his thigh. "I have to get out of them as soon as possible." Bob squirmed in his seat, trying to find a more comfortable position.

"That's a damned shame. You looked really hot in this outfit," Steve said with a smirk.

"Forget it!" Bob replied snappishly.

They drove to Bob's place in silence. Steve ordered Bob to shower first, to get warm. Then Steve used the rest of the hot water to wash all the disturbing thoughts and experiences of that evening away. His scraped-up wrists ached when the water washed away the dried blood. Once he was dry, Steve bandaged them with gauze.

"Bob, you got anything I can wear?" Steve called from the steamy bathroom.

"I put a pair of sweats right outside the bathroom door," Bob answered.

"Thanks!" Grateful, Steve dressed quickly in the soft clothes.

They sat on the couch, each in his favorite spot. Bob perched against the armrest with his legs draped over Steve's lap.

"You're still cold." Steve rubbed Bob's feet, massaging the insteps and heels. His wrists were sore, but that didn't matter as much as the close contact with Bob.

Bob rubbed his eyes. "I'm too old for this shit," he said, taking the comforter from the backrest to cover himself. In the process he put his feet on the floor.

"You sound as if you're eighty years old instead of twenty-seven."

"And I'm dog-tired." Steve yawned, resting his legs on the coffee table. "Bob?"

"Huh?" Bob looked as if he was about to fall asleep.

"You got something edible in your kitchen? My stomach's complaining." Steve put his feet down and sat up.

"You know what time it is?" Bob asked. "Almost 4:00 a.m."

"Anyway, I'm hungry. I need something really substantial, please," Steve begged.

"I could make some scrambled eggs." Bob suppressed another yawn.

"Why not? But you stay here. Let me do the work."

Steve got up. He covered Bob with the comforter, ruffling his hair before he trudged into the kitchen.

STEVE WALKED back into the living room holding two plates of scrambled eggs. He paused, looking down at the sleeping man on the couch. Bob lay on his side, one hand under his head, the other dangling down over the edge. He looked very peaceful; all the tension had faded in his sleep. Steve put the plates on the coffee table and sat across from Bob on the armchair.

What had happened to him with Randolph seemed so far away all of a sudden. Vaguely he remembered being mad at Bob but couldn't remember the exact reason for his anger. So what had he done? Lovely Luna…. Steve didn't want to think about that weekend. He had left Bob alone, and looking back, it felt like he had cheated on his best friend.

Steve thought back to when he was at the club. Several men had tried to pick him up, which he hadn't liked very much. He did like the way Bob had looked, though. The sight of Bob in his silky shirt, the tight pants, and the heeled boots had stirred something in Steve that made him uneasy.

He finished his meal with a cold beer from Bob's fridge and decided to call it a night. Bob's back would be knotted up if he slept on the couch much longer, so Steve shook him gently. "Buddy, wake up, and let's get you to bed."

Bob mumbled something unintelligible, but Steve managed to pull him up and lead him to the bedroom, where Bob slumped onto the bed. Steve didn't waste any time trying to undress him. He switched the light off and turned to go. "Sleep tight," he said, and was about to leave the room when the phone rang.

Steve stood, rooted to the spot. *Who can that be?* All of a sudden, images of Sanders and Chris trying to kill him and Bob filled his head. *If they find out we aren't dead, they might search for us, call us….*

Bob raised his head, then let it fall back on the pillow. "Get the phone, please."

Reluctantly, Steve picked up the receiver. "'Lo?"

"Is it you, Steve? Sorry for calling. I just wanted to know how your party at Steps to Heaven went."

"Larry! I can tell you, it was a hell of a night!" Steve slumped on the bed, relieved.

"I've been calling you and Bob all night, and when you didn't pick up, I just got carried away." Larry sounded breathless.

"It was a close call," Steve said, appreciating Larry's concern.

Bob nudged him. "Ask him if he has heard any news on the street."

Obviously hearing what Bob said, Larry answered, "I tried to get my brother on the phone. He goes to the downtown clubs frequently, but he isn't at home. I haven't heard anything new."

"We'll stop by to see you tomorrow," Steve said. "Thanks, Larry." Steve paused for a moment, looking down at his bandaged wrists. "Are you still in contact with Bella, your former waitress? Have you heard from Freddie?"

Larry sounded surprised. "Why d'you ask? They're running Dinah's diner, and as far as I know, it's a success."

"We'll meet tomorrow, okay?" Steve said and hung up. He took a deep breath. Remembering the precarious situation in the woods, he shuddered.

Bob put a soothing hand on Steve's knee. "We're alive. That's what matters," he said, lying back and snuggling under the covers.

Steve smiled wearily. "We should get some rest." He put his hand over Bob's. "Tomorrow we have to dig deep into Sanders's and Barber's lives, find out what makes them tick. Their financials, how they hid ownership of the club, and most importantly, where the Blue Rocket comes from."

"Would you do me a favor?" Bob asked. All of a sudden, he didn't sound sleepy.

"For you, always!" Steve stood, looking down at his partner.

"I don't want you to sleep on that lousy couch of mine." He looked up at Steve. "I don't mind if you stay here." Bob pointed to the empty side of the bed.

"You think I'm that easy?" Steve joked, but inside, he had a sudden deep affection for Bob. It made him light-headed. "I can't refuse you anything." Steve wiggled an eyebrow.

He pulled up the blanket and slid in. The thought of being this close to Bob made him feel uneasy. He wondered why, because they had shared a bed before.

However, lying next to Bob, close enough to touch, felt wonderful. The visions he'd been having of his beautiful partner took on new meaning. Steve didn't dare move, and sleep wouldn't come. Finally he turned away from Bob, careful not to hog too much of the covers.

He must have fallen asleep. When he woke, it was about 8:00 a.m. He needed to use the bathroom and slid out of bed so that he didn't disturb the sleeping Bob.

When he returned, Bob had turned on his back and was snoring lightly. Steve thought of staying awake and preparing breakfast. It was still too early, though, and he could use some more shut-eye. He lay down, but there was no space left between him and Bob. Steve squeezed under the covers and turned to his side, away from Bob. He pulled up the blanket, covering himself with the one corner not wrapped around Bob. He closed his eyes, savoring Bob's body heat.

Bob made a sound as if he were choking. He moved in his sleep, and Steve felt an arm snaking around his waist. Bob snuggled closer to spoon up against Steve.

Steve held his breath. He felt protected and safe, and at the same time, his body had quite a reaction. With Bob wrapped around him, Steve felt his own cock swelling. He really didn't want Bob to notice *that*. Abruptly Steve wriggled out of Bob's grasp. He sat up and put his feet on the ground.

"Stay," Bob said sluggishly.

Steve was drawn back into the arms of his partner. Unable to resist the temptation, he surrendered.

"I need you," Bob said.

Steve had no difficulty feeling Bob's excitement where their bodies pressed together.

"Bob...." Steve didn't know what to say or do. Maybe Bob just needed to take a leak. It was normal to have a hard-on in the morning.

But for Steve, something important had changed. He was sexually aroused by Bob's closeness. *I don't want to risk our deep friendship.*

Steve moved closer to the edge of the bed, pawing the bedside table. "Where's my watch?"

"You lost it. Remember?" Bob said softly. Without warning, he turned away from Steve and got out of bed on his side.

Steve heard the bathroom door close and sighed with relief. *That was close!* He pushed a hand under his sweatpants. He was nearly flaccid again. He almost felt disappointed. If Bob hadn't left the bed....

Uncomfortable, Steve cursed himself for being awake this early. At his own home, he could have slept undisturbed. But this close to his gorgeous partner, there was too much distraction. This new sensation was too confusing. Why did he keep noticing Bob's masculine beauty?

Steve got out of bed still in the sweats and shirt Bob had given him. The clothes he'd worn to Steps to Heaven were dirty and needed a wash. He was on his way to find something suitable in Bob's drawer when Bob came out of the bathroom, avoiding looking at him.

"I'm going for a run," Bob said, grabbing his gray jogging sweats and a black shirt.

"Any idea if I have jeans and shirts in your drawer?" Steve asked absently, concentrating on the selection of clothing. By the time he found a pair of his own worn-out jeans, Bob had gone.

"Take care...," Steve called behind him, without finishing the sentence.

He got dressed and padded down the stairwell to get the *Culver City Chronicle* on the bottom step. Unfolding it right away, he was surprised to see nothing on the front page about Steps to Heaven. Obviously there hadn't been any arrests in the night. Would Sanders and Barber be suspicious if they didn't see headlines about two dead cops? And what about Freddie? What had happened to him? Was the man who had saved him and Bob in any danger?

Steve was making coffee when Bob came back, out of breath and sweaty.

"Hey, is that my favorite T-shirt you're wearing?" Bob eyed Steve's outfit suspiciously.

"Red doesn't suit you anyway," Steve countered, tasting the hot brew.

"Very funny! What about having breakfast at Dinah's?" Bob asked before he disappeared for a shower.

"Yeah, a stack of pancakes with bacon will wake me up," Steve called after him. Maybe they would have a chance to talk to Freddie. Did Bella know her husband was working for Vice? The police must have arranged for him to be released early to go undercover for them. Would have been nice if Vice let Steve and Bob in on the operation so they didn't wind up working two different ends of the same case.

Toweling his hair dry, Bob came out of the bathroom, letting out a cloud of moist air. "Can we go?" Bob asked, tossing the towel onto the bathroom floor. His hair was still damp.

Steve watched Bob run a comb through his blond locks. Because it was still wet, the dazzling color was darker, but once it dried in the sun, it would look white blond.

"What are you looking at?" Bob grabbed his brown jacket.

"Nothing," Steve said, tipping his coffee away.

"Your gun," Bob reminded him.

Steve thanked him with a smile.

"And now, time for breakfast!" Steve rubbed his hands in anticipation when they were in the car.

"First things first. We've got to check in at the precinct," Bob said and started the engine. Steve protested weakly. "I can't work well with an empty stomach. Listen!" He hoped Bob would hear his belly rumbling.

Bob only made a face and maneuvered them safely through the heavy morning traffic.

Steve wasn't in the best mood when they entered the squad room. There was a pile of folders and papers on their desk.

Sullivan and Myers looked up from their paperwork, smirking. "Mornin'. Lots of news," Sullivan said, pointing at Rollins's office.

"I hope they found a trace of Blue Rocket and maybe even busted Sanders and Barber," Bob said, knocking at Rollins's door.

Rollins growled, "Come in!"

"Mornin', sir." Steve went over to the armchair to sit down, looking expectantly at his superior. "Can't wait to hear what the team found at Steps to Heaven last night."

"Were Sanders and Barber there?" Bob didn't sit down, as if ready to leave at a moment's notice.

"First, about the weapon you two found last night." Rollins consulted a sheet of paper. "It's still in the lab, and Ballistics is running tests. Bob's fingerprints were the only ones they found so far." He paused, flipping through some folders.

"No surprise there," Bob said dryly.

"What about the drug?" Steve asked. "Any evidence that people bought Blue Rocket at the club? Did they search the guests? Did they find the drug?" Steve got up and started pacing.

"What about Sanders and Barber? They're on the run, aren't they?" Bob asked, grabbing Steve's arm to calm him down.

Rollins looked up from the reports. "It says here that the bartender, Juan Baptiste, wasn't very cooperative when the team showed up. He hid some boxes, but eventually our team discovered the hidden evidence."

"What was in it?" Steve stared at Rollins.

"Many papers with addresses of potential users. In one of the boxes, they found more than fifty envelopes, filled with white pills. They have to be analyzed by the lab techs." Rollins exhaled loudly.

"Did they interrogate the DJ, Ronnie, and the other employees?" Bob asked. "Do they produce Blue Rocket in the club? Maybe in the back rooms?"

"Not in the club, that's for sure," Rollins said. "It looks as if they used the back rooms for introducing and selling the new drug to members of the club. But the team searched the guests and discovered some of these pills and needles to inject something."

"And Juan? How much does he know?" Steve sat down again.

"He will be interrogated and asked about his connection with Sanders and Barber today." Rollins leafed through the folder in front of him. "Right now we can charge Sanders and Barber with attempting to kill police officers, which is a federal offense. That will get them off the street, but I want more."

"We need to know where they manufactured the drug and if Sanders and Barber are also responsible for the deaths attributed to Blue Rocket overdoses," Bob said seriously.

"We have to find Sanders and Barber! They must be involved in Randolph's death." Steve stood up and went to the door.

"At the very least, they know much more than they are letting on," Bob added, following his partner. "And I suspect they lied about their alibis."

"Wait!" Rollins stopped them. "First you should have a look at the boxes they found at the club. They're in the evidence room."

"First I'd like to—" Steve began.

"Myers and Johnson are digging through them to find any trace of Sanders and his companions. You know more about this case, so it's your responsibility." With a gesture, Rollins dismissed them. "Talk to you later."

"Okay." Steve held the door open for Bob and nodded at Rollins. "See you later, Lieutenant."

THE EVIDENCE room was empty when Steve and Bob entered.

"I bet Myers and Johnson are having breakfast," Steve said, trying to ignore the rumbling of his stomach.

"So let's find something useful in these boxes, so you can get your stomach filled soon," Bob said with a smile. "I'll start with the box over there." He pointed to a table on the left.

Steve nodded and opened another box. "Bob, look what I've got here." He rummaged through some papers. "Here's a list of people, with their address, age, and the number of times they were at the club. Each date has different numbers. No idea what they mean." Steve shrugged and continued his search.

"What about how many times they bought the drug? And do the addresses match the victims who died from Blue Rocket? We'll have to check that out," Bob mumbled, fishing a brochure out of his box. "Very interesting...."

"Huh?" Steve looked up and saw the colorful flyer in Bob's hand. "What is it?"

"It's an ad for Dr. Glassman's beauty clinic in Santa Barbara."

"Really? It's not unusual for a beauty surgeon to advertise his business in a club like this one." Steve frowned. "Do you think he's involved somehow?"

"He would have access to a lab where Blue Rocket could be manufactured," Bob mused. "As a doctor, no one would think twice if he bought the chemicals and equipment...."

"You could be right. Rollins said they found no evidence of drug making in the club. Dr. Glassman—" Steve snapped his fingers. "We're going to search Glassman's office."

"No private parties, remember?" Bob added, looking for more useful material in the box in front of him.

"I'm going to call Rollins right away." Steve rushed over to a phone and dialed.

Chapter Twelve

"ROLLINS IS going to ask for some backup from police headquarters in Santa Barbara," Steve said, heading down to the garage. "He'll get a warrant from Judge Stanley to search Glassman's office, so we have a little time." He rubbed his belly. "I wanna have breakfast. Let's hurry over to Dinah's."

"Hopefully after breakfast we'll have the warrant and the backup will be in place, ready to move in to search the doctor's office." Bob frowned. "I wonder if Freddie's okay."

"Bella will tell us, buddy," Steve said, fighting as usual to open the door of the Thunderbird.

When Steve and Bob entered Dinah's diner, it was so busy they had to spend more time looking for a free table. The morning atmosphere was bright and friendly, which obviously appealed to the breakfast crowd. That and the special coupons that had run in the morning newspaper.

"Over there." Steve pointed at a table just as three young men got up to leave. Steve took a seat with a grin and opened the menu.

Bob sat next to him. "I haven't seen Bella. Do you think she knows what her husband is involved in?"

"Were you talking about me?" Bella came up behind them. "Good morning, Steve and Bob."

"Hi, Bella, how are things going?" Bob said, trying not to sound worried. "My partner is starving, so your special breakfast for him, please."

"Good boy," Steve said appreciatively. He patted Bella's hand. "Sweetie, we'd like to talk with Freddie. We could use his help with a case."

Bella fumbled with her notepad. "Get in line. I need to talk with him too. He didn't come home last night, but he phoned and said he had met some old friends." She sighed. "It just didn't sound right. He told me not to worry, that he was staying out of town. But I do worry. I hope he isn't in trouble." She looked at her wristwatch. "I'm expecting him back at any minute."

Bob put his hand on her arm. "Don't worry, Bella. He'll be back, I'm sure." He glanced at Steve and saw the same hope reflected in his eyes. The last thing they wanted was another murder on their hands.

Freddie didn't appear while they were having breakfast, and Bella looked increasingly concerned.

STEVE AND Bob were on the freeway toward Santa Barbara right after their breakfast. Rollins had arranged everything with the police there. They were supposed to meet a couple of uniformed officers in a black-and-white near the Glassman office.

"I was just thinking," Steve said, turning the steering wheel. He revved up to pass a slow-moving VW bug, glad for a section of freeway without much traffic. At this rate, they would arrive there in no time. "In his statement Sanders said he was with Gloria Thumbnail last Wednesday, and she insisted that they spent every Wednesday together. And that they went to talk to Glassman on Wednesday, but a traffic jam made them late." He looked at Bob. "We need to talk to her again."

Bob nodded, putting on his sunglasses against the bright sun. "Dr. Glassman confirmed that Sanders and Gloria Thumbnail visited him on Wednesday."

"Don't believe what the doctor says," Steve said sarcastically, watching the road when he wanted to watch his partner.

Bob pinched his nose. "Whatever the truth is, we have to find Sanders and Barber." Impatiently he drummed his fingers against the frame of the side window. "I sure hope we get some hard evidence that

Glassman is involved with making Blue Rocket, or we're back to square one." He sighed.

Steve felt the urge to take Bob in his arms to comfort him and assure him how much he cared, but he forced himself to concentrate on the task ahead. And he was driving.

They were at a crossroads. With the evidence they had they could tie Sanders and Barber into the mix. But their specific role in the manufacture and sale of Blue Rocket wasn't clear, only that they had tried to kill Steve and Bob, and possibly Randolph. Not to mention, what had been their motives? He'd sure love to see Sanders and Barber when they found out that the men they had tried to kill were still alive. And what about Freddie? Had Sanders and Barber discovered his duplicity?

"I hope Freddie is okay," Bob said that moment.

It made Steve smile fondly. They often had the same thoughts at the same time. "I've just been thinking of him. I hope so too."

TWO HOURS later Steve and Bob reached Santa Barbara. Steve drove past the white office building, slowed down, and came to a halt at the end of the block. "I don't want them to see us too early." Steve opened the door and got out.

Bob had taken off his sunglasses. Now he squinted as he climbed out of the car. "Our backup must be somewhere here. I'll take a look around the next corner." Bob walked across the road with long strides. Steve followed close behind him.

"There they are!" Bob saw a police car next to a garden hedge.

A tall black man got out of the car. "Detectives Bob Curry and Steve Randall? I'm Sergeant Alan Mercer." Mercer reached out to shake their hands. "This is my partner, Officer Roberto Garcia."

A man with short dark hair joined them. He straightened his uniform and shook hands with the detectives.

"Good to know you." Steve nodded. "Glassman is the main suspect in a drug operation. We don't want to spook him. Why don't Mercer and I go to the back door while Garcia stays with Bob to secure the entrance?"

"Sounds good to me," Mercer agreed, pushing his blue cap back further on his head.

"Be careful," Bob said quietly to Steve, his arm lingering just a second longer than necessary on Steve's back.

"You play the good cop. Good luck." A pat on Bob's stomach, and Steve was gone.

Bob took a deep breath. So much had happened in the past week. He hoped they were about to solve the case. There were so many questions left. Had Glassman really manufactured the drug? If so, had he used his contacts with Sanders to distribute Blue Rocket through Steps to Heaven? Had he ever been involved in other illegal drug sales?

Bob waited until Steve and Mercer had faded away around the back of the white building before he marched across the road with Garcia in tow. This was it. The lobby looked quiet, and he didn't sense that Glassman was expecting the police.

"Hi." Bob walked up to the reception desk.

Debbie Schellenberg, the same girl he had seen last time, was working at the computer. Her long red fingernails scraped the keyboard, and she didn't look up when Bob rapped his knuckles on the counter.

"CCPD," Bob said firmly, holding his badge out to her. "We need to talk to Dr. Glassman. It's important."

"Oh!" Debbie stopped typing. "I didn't notice...." She looked around and saw the officer outside. Reaching under the counter, she appeared to press a hidden button.

An alarm of some sort?

She smiled up at Bob. "I remember you! Sorry, but Dr. Glassman isn't available today. He has a meeting at the hospital. Can I take a message?"

Bob gestured for Garcia to come inside. "We have a warrant to search Dr. Glassman's offices. Wait here until we're done. Officer Garcia will stay with you."

Debbie made a small squeak of protest.

Bob stared her down. "After that, I have some questions for you too."

He started with the exam rooms on the first floor. There were gurneys and medical equipment, but otherwise the rooms were empty. He saw no patients and no medical staff doing any work. He and Debbie seemed to be the only ones in the building, which was odd. Bob went up to the second floor but found that too abandoned. He didn't find anything that looked like a laboratory where Glassman could make drugs.

"Where's the drug lab?" Bob asked himself. He went back down to the lobby.

Guarded by Garcia, Debbie looked at Bob, wide eyed. "What's going on?" she shrieked.

"Debbie, what's down below here?"

"Dr. Glassman's private rooms," she said with a pout, and then sucked on her bottom lip. "But I've never been there. Only he's allowed inside."

"Show me the way," Bob said. "Garcia, come with us. Keep your eye on Debbie, so she doesn't try to bolt." Bob looked around but couldn't see Steve and Mercer. *Where are they?*

Bob drew his pistol and went downstairs, pointing it ahead of him. He was astonished to see how large the basement was. There was a wide, brightly illuminated hall lined with doors on both sides.

Bob looked back at Debbie. She had an unreadable expression. "Knock on the first door, and call for your boss," he said to her quietly.

"You guard the rear," he told Garcia.

Debbie hesitated only a moment before rapping at the door. "Doctor?"

When nobody answered, Bob tried the knob and opened the door. The room was empty. It looked like an operating room, with medical equipment on both sides of an operating table.

The next rooms looked abandoned as well. An unnatural silence lay over the floor. Bob had the feeling that Glassman, Sanders, and Barber weren't here.

"What about this room?" Garcia stopped in front of the last room at the end of the floor, his weapon ready, clenched tightly in his fist. "Private" said the red letters on a sign.

"This is Dr. Glassman's lab, no one is allowed in," Debbie said, biting her bottom lip.

Bob nodded curtly, anxious to find his partner. His internal alarm was jangling because Steve hadn't checked in with him after going around the back of the building.

"Call your boss again," he commanded, frowning at Debbie.

Her voice quavered. "Dr. Glassman?"

Again there was no answer. Debbie cautiously opened the door and stepped in, with Bob and Garcia on her heels.

A hand shot out from behind the door and throttled her, pulling her backward. Bob stopped, scanning the room in an instant. Glassman held his receptionist against him with a gun to her ribs. Sanders was in the middle of the room with a small scalpel to Steve's throat. Steve's hands were tied in front with plastic cable, but his blue eyes blazed angrily. Bob couldn't see obvious wounds, thank God. Mercer, on the other hand, lay unconscious in the corner by the sink.

"What the fuck did you do to my partner?" Bob took a step forward, leveling his weapon at the doctor.

The room was a functional lab, full of test tubes, beakers, Bunsen burners, and vials of blue powder. There was an acrid smell in the air, and if the boxes piled by the door were any indication, Glassman had been in the process of trying to escape with his wares—possibly Blue Rocket?

"I wouldn't do that," Ruben Glassman said from the left, using Debbie as a shield.

"Mercer," Garcia said softly, glancing at the other people and holding his gun away from his body. Obviously concerned for his partner, he sidled around the sink and started to kneel beside Mercer.

"Don't move!" Glassman pulled the trigger. The bullet hit the wall only inches from Garcia's head. He froze, glaring at the doctor.

"Where's Freddie Garner and Chris Barber?" Bob asked, trying desperately to maneuver a clear shot at either Sanders or Glassman, but from his angle, it was impossible.

"Freddie is a dead man now," Sanders said savagely. "Chris went to check on the dead bodies in North Park and took Freddie with him. Bad luck for traitors."

Steve gritted his teeth, glaring at his captor.

"Shut up!" Glassman shouted at Sanders, forcing Debbie across the room by pushing her along with his pistol.

"Doc, you're a clever man," Bob said, watching Steve for any sign of a plan. "But you'll go to San Quentin for the rest of your life, when we prove that you created Blue Rocket. Too many young people died because of your drug."

"You haven't proven anything yet, and there's no way a jury will convict me in a drug addict's death!" Glassman laughed, waving his pistol around his lab. "Nobody do anything stupid, or somebody will die," he threatened, pushing the gun against Debbie's ribs again. She cried out, terrified, but he snarled at her, and she clamped her lips closed. "Sorry about the whole mess, gentlemen, but I was just about to leave." He glanced over at several boxes by the door.

Bob couldn't take his eyes off Steve, but he would have loved to know what was in the boxes. Steve mouthed his name, shifting his weight very slightly against Sanders as if trying to slide out of the way. Sanders lowered his hand with the scalpel and squeezed Steve's arm to keep him upright.

"Sorry, Ruben, I know who's responsible for this mess," Sanders growled. "If Freddie, that piece of shit, had done his job as expected, we wouldn't have to deal with these two wannabe heroes." He flicked the blade of the scalpel along Steve's skin, causing blood to trickle down his throat.

Bob knew exactly what Steve wanted to do, and he didn't like it. He could almost hear his partner's voice. *I'll go limp, and you shoot the asshole behind me.*

It was a dangerous plan. Steve was close enough to Sanders that he could easily be hit by a stray bullet. And there was no guarantee that Garcia would be able to wing Glassman at the same time, especially with Debbie in the way.

"Doctor!" Debbie wailed. "Why are you doing this? What's going on?"

"Shut up." He dragged her to the door and pushed her roughly against a cupboard full of lab supplies. Debbie sobbed.

Concerned, Garcia turned, keeping Mercer behind him. "You'll never get away with this. The local police are sending another team."

Bob lowered his weapon as if he was giving up. "Garcia, we can't fight them, not with the possibility of anyone else getting hurt."

At that moment Steve went limp in Sanders's arms. Surprised, Sanders nearly dropped the scalpel.

Faster than he had ever done on the shooting range, Bob raised his weapon and fired once. The bullet tore through Sanders's shoulder, and he reflexively gripped the scalpel harder, plunging it into Steve's right arm.

With a yelp of pain, Sanders clutched at his shoulder. Steve gasped, trying to roll away from his attacker.

"You bastard!" Glassman pointed his weapon at Bob, shoving Debbie out of the way. She tumbled into the pile of boxes.

Garcia swung his service revolver up with perfect form, shooting Glassman's pistol out of his hand.

"You have the right to remain silent!" Bob roared, swinging Glassman against a nearby desk chair to cuff his arms behind him. Glassman cried out in pain, and blood from his injured hand dripped to the floor. Bob recited the Miranda warnings as fast as humanly possible, his eyes on Steve.

"Dispatch?" Garcia pulled his walkie-talkie off his utility belt. "We need backup here, pronto. And a couple of ambulances."

"Bob, get Sanders!" Steve called, trying to scoot as far away from Sanders as possible. "He's a squirrelly one."

"Can't you see I have my hands full?" Bob yelled, kicking Glassman's gun out of the way. He was just glad Steve was still talking, although there was a lot of blood on his arm.

"What's going on?" Mercer awoke and looked around, dazed.

"I gotta get out of here!" Debbie moaned, crouching by the door. "I don't want this job anymore!"

"You missed all the action." Garcia knelt by his partner's side, checking for injuries. "What did they do to you?"

"I got a blow to the head, went down," Mercer mumbled, holding his head.

"Clumsy oaf. I'll be right back. Got to escort the good doctor out for his ride to lockup." Briefly Garcia patted Mercer's arm.

"See you later, then, partner," Mercer said with a sigh.

"Come on, Doc." Garcia hauled Glassman up and out of the lab with savage glee.

"I have rights! This is an outrage!" Glassman yelled.

"Your right is to shut up," Steve hissed, trying to get up from the floor. He failed, his face contorted with pain.

"Your turn, shitface." Bob hauled Sanders up, not caring in the least that he had shot the man in the shoulder. He turned Sanders to the wall, snapping the cuffs on him. "Steve? You all right?"

Steve gave him a pale but game thumbs-up, and Bob felt like he could breathe easily for the first time since entering the office. He shook his captive. "John Sanders, we've got you on kidnapping, assault on a police officer, and a host of other charges that will keep you in the slammer for years." Bob grinned nastily, about to launch into the Miranda warnings again.

"Still in love with each other?" Sanders sneered over his shoulder. "Your careers will be over the moment that gets out!"

"So will yours," Bob said curtly, propelling Sanders to the door. "The department doesn't take too kindly to people who try to kill their officers."

"Or who kill people like Randolph," Steve spoke up.

"Faggot cops!" Sanders shouted. "Randy had to pay for what he wanted to do to us, and now…." He groaned, gasping as Bob shoved him into the arms of two uniformed police officers who came running down the hall.

Steve tried to sit up straighter, holding on to his bleeding arm. "Damn, this was my favorite shirt."

"I'll get you a new one," Bob said, well aware that when Steve complained a lot, his wound wasn't too bad. He grabbed a cloth from beside the lab sink and wrapped it tightly around Steve's arm. "Put pressure on that."

"You don't have to tell me." Steve winced, looking down at the makeshift bandage.

Garcia came back. "Ambulance is here." He went over to his partner with a fond grin. "Hey, Mercer, you want to get up by yourself or are you going to lie here all day?"

"I thought I'd leave all the grunt work to you, Roberto," Mercer tried to laugh but rubbed his forehead ruefully.

"Here's your limo ride to County!" Garcia waved a hand at a pair of paramedics.

They brought in a gurney and trundled Mercer out quickly.

"Sorry it worked out this way, Bob and Steve. I'll call you with details later on." Garcia trailed along behind, talking softly to his partner.

"Thanks," Steve called after him.

"Debbie," Bob said softly, "you need to go get checked out at the hospital. You've had quite a scare today."

"I can't believe Dr. Glassman tried to kill me!" she wailed. "He owes me. He promised me plastic surgery on my nose if I kept my mouth shut about whatever he was doing in that lab! I had a signed paper somewhere in my desk...."

"You're beautiful just the way you are," Bob told her. He wanted to look for that document, which would go a long way to proving Glassman's guilt.

"Come on, miss," a young paramedic said quietly. He helped her out just as the room filled with more uniformed cops, the lab crew, and another pair of paramedics.

"Glassman was trying to leave with those boxes," Bob said to the head of the lab guys. "Check the contents first. And there are probably traces of Blue Rocket all over this room."

"Looks like you've lost a little blood." A dark-haired paramedic knelt down beside Steve to take care of the wound. "What about your neck? There's blood." The paramedic checked the injury and then smiled reassuringly. "Only a scratch. I'll apply a plaster."

"Thanks." Steve put more pressure on his wounded arm. It had nearly stopped bleeding. "And this is no big deal either. I can slap a Band-Aid on it once I get home."

Bob shook his head, leveling a long finger at his partner. "See you at the hospital. I'm going to inform Rollins. They have to find Barber and Freddie before something terrible happens."

"Take care of my black lady," Steve whispered as a paramedic led him out of the room. "She's a spoiled beauty."

"With doors that won't open properly," Bob muttered, following him outside. The building was ringed with black-and-whites and emergency vehicles of every sort belonging to the Santa Barbara cops.

Steve threw a sour smile over his shoulder before climbing into the ambulance. "I have to fix that little problem." He sat down on a gurney for the ride. "Don't be late, huh?"

Steve sounded like a lost little boy. Bob would have loved to show him how much he cared. But not in public. He patted Steve's hand and stood back to let the paramedic close the doors to the ambulance. Bob frowned, watching it leave, then headed back inside to help with the cleanup and to look for the paper Debbie had mentioned. He wanted to get to Steve as quickly as possible and drive him back to Culver City so that he could take care of him. How exactly had Sanders and Glassman gotten the better of Steve and Mercer anyway?

Chapter Thirteen

"THAT'S GOOD news," Bob said and nodded, even though Rollins couldn't see a nod over the phone. "Yes, I'm with Steve at the hospital. Fortunately there was only a scratch on his neck, but his arm needed eight stitches. Otherwise he's fine." He glanced over at Steve, sitting on an examination table, cradling his injured right arm.

"It still hurts like hell, Bob! And I won't be able to write reports for weeks!" Steve complained.

"Yeah, I know, he's always like that." Bob laughed at Rollins's response and hung up.

"You'll be yourself again in no time." Bob smiled and helped Steve off the gurney and toward a wheelchair. "Anything I can do for you?"

"I can walk on my own." Steve shoved the wheelchair aside. "I wanna go home. Nothing else."

"Your wish is my command." Bob eyed Steve's sling, making sure he was wearing it correctly. "Let's get out of here."

Slowly they went to the reception desk to sign the needed release papers.

When Steve saw the black Thunderbird, he grinned from ear to ear. He ran his free hand along the bright hood. "Beauty, did Bob treat you well? No dents, no damage?"

"Shut up, and get in!" Bob ordered, smiling inwardly. He had to admit that Steve's car had become special to him too.

On his way to the hospital, his thoughts had centered on the many funny and exciting incidents they'd had in the car. He didn't even want to imagine how often Steve had had sex in his precious car. He must have done the deed last weekend, when Bob was all by himself. Steve's car had smelled awful afterward, with whatever he'd sprayed inside to attract his date.

Bob couldn't hide his own jealousy. It was ridiculous! There was nothing wrong if Steve wanted to make out in his car with a hot lady.

"Is something bothering you?" Steve nudged him with his good arm.

"It's nothing. I just thought I could get used to driving your car." Bob looked straight ahead at the traffic in front of them on the freeway. He concentrated on steering through the rush of cars.

"I knew it! But after today I'm fed up driving around so much. I want a couple of quiet hours at home with no one molesting me, no one trying to kill me, and no more cases to work on." Steve yawned.

Bob realized how exhausted Steve must be. He wanted to ask why he and Mercer had gotten into trouble at the back entrance of Glassman's office, but one look at Steve's tired face told him to postpone the question. All that mattered was that they had done a successful job in Santa Barbara. Everything else could wait until morning.

When they arrived at Steve's street, Bob slowed down to make the turn into Steve's driveway.

Steve opened his eyes. "Home, sweet home," he said softly when Bob switched off the ignition.

"You want to be alone? I can take a cab home," Bob said, uncertainly.

Steve looked at him, his eyes a dark shade of blue. "A taxi? I have a pizza in the freezer you can eat, and I'm sure there's still a few beers, so… can I coax you into staying with me?"

"Aren't you hungry?" Bob was surprised.

"Not really." Steve tried to open the passenger door with his left arm—and failed.

"Wait! I'll help you." Bob was around the car in no time. He yanked the car door open and took Steve's uninjured elbow to help him out.

"I'm not an invalid, you know," Steve protested, but he didn't object when Bob put his arm around his waist to steady him. Instead, he looked at Bob with an unreadable expression.

"Let's get that pizza warmed up," Bob said when they got into the apartment. He went into the kitchen while Steve disappeared into the bathroom.

Bob was about to open a can of peaches for dessert when he heard loud cursing. Sure that he knew what the trouble was, he ran over to the room where Steve was. "You need some assistance?" he asked and opened the door. Steve stood in front of the toilet with his jeans down around his hips.

"Last time it was your hair, now you need help taking a leak?" Bob joked, entering the room.

"Damn! I can't get those jeans up and zip them!" Steve's face was red with anger. He fumbled one-handed with the belt that was stuck between his jeans and underwear.

"Didn't I tell you to buy your jeans—"

"I know, I know. Would you help me now?" Steve asked impatiently.

Bob knew Steve was embarrassed to be so vulnerable. He didn't say another word, just grabbed the jeans and pulled them up.

"Hey, careful with the equipment there!" Steve adjusted himself with his left hand, and Bob zipped the jeans in a swift movement.

"Thanks." Steve washed his hands and finger combed through his hair one-handed.

Half an hour later, they sat in front of their emptied plates, and each had two cans of beer in front of him.

"I can't tell you how glad I am to be at home. I wouldn't have survived one more minute in the ER," Steve said intensely.

"Don't you miss all those pretty nurses taking care of you?" Bob expected Steve to waggle his eyebrows with some story about all the phone numbers he had collected from nurses over the years.

Steve didn't say a word. He got up to take the plates into the kitchen.

"What happened to you and Mercer? How did Sanders and Glassman take you hostage?" Bob called after him.

"Very easily." Steve came back and sat down in his rattan rocking chair opposite the coffee table. "Somebody must have warned them. Mercer and I entered the building through the back door and didn't see anybody." He rocked back and forth, cradling his sling with his left hand. "We went down the stairs and tried a couple of the doors. We thought the lab was empty, but Glassman was lying in wait and clocked Mercer on the noggin. He dropped immediately. Before I could draw my piece, Sanders caught me from behind. That's it." Steve sounded defeated and closed his eyes.

"I thought I saw Debbie hit a hidden alarm button." Bob grimaced, thinking back. "She told me she didn't know what was going on down there but that Glassman had promised her plastic surgery in exchange for her silence."

Steve nodded absently.

"Now we have to know...." Bob stopped when he realized that Steve had fallen asleep in his chair. The injured arm pressing against his chest, he lay against the cushions with a little frown.

Maybe his arm was still hurting. Bob wasn't sure if Steve had taken his painkillers after they left the hospital. He hadn't wanted to nag him about it because Steve was a grown man, fully capable of managing life on his own.

Bob took another hearty drink from his beer. Had he overstepped some boundary with Steve? They had become close friends, nothing wrong with that. But something between them had changed. Bob sat up straighter, the beer can held in midair.

Images of Steve dancing in a disco, hips moving to the rhythm, sweat on his tanned skin.... Bob had enjoyed watching Steve. He'd give anything to change places with one of the ladies Steve dated.

How would it feel to be seduced by that good-looking guy with the infectious smile? His heart would melt. Bob felt his heartbeat speed up. For the first time, he accepted that Steve meant much more to him than just a close friend and partner.

Steve never needed much personal space. He was affectionate, always giving out hugs and slaps on the back. Bob used to be uncomfortable with such displays in public. As a kid he had learned that men weren't supposed to be so demonstrative. In fact, his family did not do strong emotion. He'd learned to keep his feelings inside. Exactly the opposite of loud, brash Steve.

How things had changed! Bob liked the way Steve was and had come to love Steve's touches and hugs. He'd even learned to give as good as he got. A small pat on the belly went a long way. Having Steve lean in close was one of the best things on earth. So why did Bob feel so unsettled? Like something was out of place? Wrong?

Bob stood up and took the empty beer cans into the kitchen. Standing by the window, he looked down on the dark street. The view was as familiar to him as the one from his own apartment. They stayed over at each other's so often that both places had become home. He didn't want to guess how many of his pants and shirts were in Steve's drawer.

He'd gotten too dependent on his pal. He remembered last week when Steve said that they spent so much time together that he wasn't getting laid often enough and had wanted to spend the weekend alone. Which was fine, except Bob had found himself lonely. Without Steve he didn't know what to do.

They usually hung around together, went to the movies or had dinner before spending the evening watching TV or playing a game of chess. Bob always won, which was probably why Steve hadn't wanted to play recently.

Deep in his heart, Bob knew that his love for his partner had crossed the line from friendship to a love he couldn't quite explain. Was he in love with Steve? Embarrassed, Bob recalled his hard-on in the hotel when he'd woke up curled against Steve. Steve must have noticed, which was why he had jerked away.

That was all the proof Bob needed to know that Steve didn't have the same feelings for him. Bob had to make some important changes in his life. The thought of leaving Steve made him feel sick, but it was necessary.

He went back to the living room, thinking about going home to leave Steve alone. But he didn't have the heart to do it. Steve was hurt. Someone should be nearby if he was in pain in the night. Bob had always been that someone in the past, and he didn't want to relinquish his role.

He sighed. It wasn't going to be easy to pull back from such a relationship. He slumped on the couch and picked up a car magazine— just one of Steve's many interests. Bob smiled when he found a dog-eared page marking an article on how to attach a spoiler to a sports car.

You should fix your car doors! He realized how often he had criticized Steve about his eating habits, his manners, and anything Bob thought of as odd. No wonder Steve was fed up with his know-it-all attitude.

They could stay friends, but it would never be anything more than that. Bob would never reveal his feelings to Steve.

He shook his head. Tomorrow, he would take the next step in his life and withdraw from Steve. Flipping through the magazine, Bob calmed down. Now that he had decided, he would hold a vigil for the last time, just in case Steve woke up and needed something.

"COME TO bed. Your back is going to kill you."

Bob heard the words in his dream. He felt a warm hand trailing up and down his arm. With all his senses, he fought the caress. "No, I have to go. Don't touch me." He pushed the hand away, afraid to surrender to the affection. No more, Steve, no more dependency. "Leave me alone. I don't need you. I...."

"Bullshit! You need me as much as I need you."

Bob could now hear Steve very clearly. *It isn't a dream.* He opened his eyes to see a pair of dark blue eyes only inches away from his face. Steve grinned, his disheveled hair hanging over his forehead.

Bob took a deep breath. It was time to confess his new plan. "Steve...," he croaked. Avoiding Steve's intense look, Bob cleared his throat. "You have to know that I can't go on this way." He saw the bandage on Steve's arm and touched it lightly. *Damn, I have to stop caring!*

"I will give you more space to live your life the way you always wanted. I'll bow out for the time being." He ducked his head so that he wouldn't have to see his pain reflected in Steve's eyes. "And now I'm going home." Only half awake, Bob struggled to get up, shoving Steve aside.

"I read somewhere that home is where the heart is," Steve said plaintively.

Refusing to listen, Bob looked around for his jacket. "I see you're fine, so let me go." He had no car. He'd have to call a cab.

"Stay here! I don't get you. Why do you want to leave now?" Although handicapped because of his bandaged arm, Steve latched onto Bob and would not let go.

Against his will Bob stared into Steve's eyes.

Bob's desperation must have shown, because Steve cupped Bob's cheek with his good hand and said quietly, "What has happened to the Bob I know? Who are you, leaving a wounded man in the middle of the night?"

Steve looked so sad that Bob laughed bitterly. "Don't tempt me, buddy. I realize that we've become much too close. It's time for a change." For a moment he leaned into Steve's hand against his cheek, then withdrew.

"You're right," Steve said. "Have a seat, and listen."

Dazed, Bob sat down on the couch. Steve took a seat right next to him, leaving no space between them. Bob tried to shift away from the familiar closeness, but Steve wouldn't let him.

"During the last couple of weeks, I've realized what went wrong in my life," Steve said, placing his hand on Bob's knee.

Don't do that! Bob wanted to cry, but no sound came out of his mouth. Instead he said, "I know I've been getting on your nerves and spoiling your free time." Steve's hand on his leg irritated him, and he tried to shove it away.

Steve grabbed Bob's hand in a strong grip. "You've got it all wrong. But I figured out something very important that I didn't see was right in front of me."

"If you want to get philosophical, this is not the right time and place." Bob pushed Steve away, shoving him back on the couch.

"Don't you see?" Steve turned to him, moving his good arm in an arc between them. "We belong together. I need you!"

"What did they give you at the hospital? You must be high. You don't know what you're saying." Bob didn't want to believe what Steve had said.

"I'll have to show you my own way." Steve snaked his left arm around Bob's neck and pulled him close.

"What the hell are you—?" Bob started, but he was cut off as his mouth was covered by soft lips. *Steve is kissing me!*

Time stood still. All Bob could sense was his heart skipping a beat. He had never felt this way. Not with any of the beautiful girls he had ever kissed. He thought he had known love before but was dead wrong until this moment in time.

Chapter Fourteen

STEVE DREW back with a smile.

Bob opened his mouth, still feeling the impression of Steve's lips on his. "My God...."

"Hit me, leave me, but know that I love you, more than my life," Steve said, his gaze fixed on Bob's.

"I-I don't get it. Lately, you've been so standoffish, telling me to get out of your life." Bob knew he sounded accusatory, but he needed to explain exactly how rejected he'd felt.

"Bob, I just couldn't see that all I wanted was right in front of me," Steve said ruefully.

"And what was the problem two days ago when we woke up in the motel and you couldn't get away from me fast enough?" Bob hadn't finished yet.

Steve blushed. "I really don't want to talk about it." He paused as if searching for the right words.

"Why?" Bob insisted.

"You turned me on, and I couldn't admit it. Capeesh?" Steve said almost defiantly, pretending to check the bandage on his right arm.

"Is that true?" Bob had been aroused too, spooned against Steve. And he was now as well.

"You have my word on it. Give me a chance to show you that I really love you, with all my heart." Steve smiled mischievously. "And my body."

Bob felt his cheeks go warm. Could it be true that Steve loved him the way he loved Steve? He didn't know how to describe what he was feeling, but he couldn't let this chance pass by.

"You're an ass, you know that?" Bob countered.

With little effort, Steve pulled Bob up to his feet and pointed to the bedroom. "After you." He unbuttoned his shirt on the way and struggled with the sling. "Holy shit! Undressing one-armed isn't fun," Steve whined and held out his arm so Bob could assist him.

Bob was still in a daze. Was this really happening? Steve had had feelings for him all along, just as he had for Steve? How could he have been so blind? How could they both! Especially when they had been sharing the same bed and both tried to hide their arousal. It was almost comical. Suddenly Bob saw the humor in the whole thing and started to laugh.

Steve grinned, still holding out his arm.

This is actually going to happen! With a joyous heart, Bob divested his partner of his sling and his shirt.

And his pants.

Then his own shirt and slacks.

When they were standing in their underwear, Bob surveyed Steve's cotton-covered erection. All for him. Excitement and panic fluttered in his belly, but he knew what to do. "Lie down and get under the covers. Be careful with your arm," he ordered.

"Thanks, Dr. Curry. Where's my medicine?" Steve snuggled under the blanket until only his dark hair was visible.

"I don't know where you keep the painkillers." Bob looked around. "Are they in the bag we brought home from the hospital?"

"Dummy, *you* are my painkiller. Switch off the light, and join me." Steve stuck his good arm out of the covers to coax Bob into the bed.

Slowly Bob pulled back the covers and slid into bed.

"You're cold," Steve said, putting his arms around Bob's waist.

"That'll change in no time." Bob relaxed into Steve's embrace. Steve's dark hair made a nice contrast on the white pillow. The look on his face was so loving Bob couldn't resist bending down to give him a kiss. "You mind?"

"Not a bit. In fact, I insist," Steve murmured.

What followed was a gentle exploration of lips, their stubbled cheeks rubbing against each other. Bob was careful not to jostle Steve's injured arm.

"You're the best painkiller, Bob." Steve smiled, tangling his fingers in Bob's hair. "If Sanders hadn't knifed me, I would be able to show what loving you means to me." Steve let his hand wander down, trailing soft circles on Bob's chest.

Bob held his breath and stifled a moan when Steve's hand roamed over his nipple, which hardened under his touch. This was such an arousing sensation Bob was tempted to push Steve's hand aside. It was almost too much.

"You like it, and I like doing it to you." Steve moved his hand farther down, resting it on Bob's stomach and then tracing his navel in soothing circles.

When Steve started to go below his navel, Bob tensed. "No," he said, full of mixed emotions. He wanted Steve ready for more action, but not until his arm was better. "Right now, I just want to be close to you, holding you and feeling you by my side. This way." Bob lay down again, putting his arm over Steve's waist and leaning into his solid body.

"Looking forward to another day with my soon-to-be lover." Steve turned his head to Bob, and they shared another deep kiss. Wrapped in each other's arms, silence surrounded them, and Bob drifted off into a peaceful sleep.

BOB WOKE to the sound of running water in the bathroom. He lay on his back, moving his arm across the empty side of the bed. It was still warm, so Steve must have left only a few minutes ago.

Bob forced his eyes open and looked at the alarm clock on the nightstand: 6:00 a.m. Normally he was up at this time of the day to take his usual run along the beach. But today everything was different. It was hard to believe that he had been ready to leave Steve last night. Instead they had spent the night together. Not head to toe like in the hotel but embracing, like lovers. Bob had not slept so deeply in a long time.

He stretched, and his long legs touched the end of the brass bed. He moved up against the headboard and looked around. Clothes were spread everywhere on the floor. Steve would probably complain about the mess they'd made. Bob chuckled. Steve was the neatnik who was always tidying up. Bob never minded when there was trash in the backseat of his car or sheets of music all over his coffee table.

Here at Steve's place, generally, everything was put away neatly. Except this morning.

Steve came out of the bathroom adjusting his briefs one-handed. He wasn't even wearing his sling.

Bob had just opened his mouth to ask where it was when Steve smiled broadly at him.

"How was your night, love? I slept like a log." Steve grinned, swaggering to the bed. "I didn't need your help with my morning routine. Luckily I wasn't wearing any jeans that had to be unzipped."

"I could get used to you without any pants," Bob said lustfully.

Laughing, Steve jumped onto the bed, making the mattress bounce up and down.

"Take care of your arm!" Bob warned, just before Steve dived into his lap.

Steve grinned up at Bob, his blue eyes sparkling. "I'm better, Bob. Look!" He moved his arm in front of Bob's face. "It doesn't hurt anymore. At least I don't feel bad when I'm near you."

Bob's cock responded to having Steve so close. "Lemme go for a moment. You know, morning routine." Bob smiled apologetically, responding to the call of his full bladder. He was still too embarrassed to let Steve see his hard-on.

"Sure. Let me have a look at that beauty first." Steve pulled the covers away from Bob's body to reveal the impressive bulge in Bob's shorts. "I love it… and I love you too," he whispered, searching Bob's mouth for a kiss.

Bob surrendered to Steve's loving words. He met Steve's lips, savoring the sweetness, and could have stayed this way forever… but he needed to use the bathroom. "Be right back," he said, his belly fluttering with nervousness.

When Bob returned to the bedroom, the covers almost completely hid Steve. Bob lifted up the blanket and saw Steve's feet tangled in the sheets. As gently as a feather's touch, he ran a finger along the sole of Steve's foot.

"Argh." Steve kicked out and rolled to the side to get away from the tickling.

Bob grabbed Steve's legs to calm him down. Steve chuckled, turning onto his stomach. Bob crawled back into bed. He slid his hands down Steve's muscular calves and thighs. Steve just about purred from Bob's caresses. Bob still felt like he was rediscovering everything about arousal. This was Steve, his body so familiar but so new.

Bob positioned himself between Steve's legs. He pulled down Steve's tight briefs. "You are beautiful," Bob whispered, admiring Steve.

"Good things come to him who waits," Steve snickered. He held his breath when Bob put his hand on Steve's buttocks, lingering there.

"And I've been waiting a long time for this," Bob said in a low voice. "And it's a very nice view from here." He grabbed one buttock and kneaded it. The cleft between Steve's butt cheeks was tight. Fascinated, Bob lowered his head and kissed the warm flesh there. Carefully, he pulled Steve's asscheeks apart to do some further exploration.

Steve moaned, and Bob stopped immediately. He never thought he would be able to be that intimate with his best friend.

Steve shifted to lie on his side. Bob slid to Steve's front. He mumbled, "Sorry. Got carried away."

"Nothing to be sorry about. I just wanted to see your face." Their lips met for another kiss.

Bob was still in the mood for some exploration, and he let his tongue trail along Steve's lips.

Tongues mingled, and they tasted each other's flavor. Bob couldn't get enough of Steve. Finally he drew back and moaned, "That was priceless."

"Ditto." Steve licked his lips as if he wanted to save Bob's taste on his mouth. "Let me see you," he said, his eyes dark and full of desire.

When Bob hesitated Steve pushed the covers away. He lay naked in front of Bob, his cock aroused and ready for action.

"Now you," Steve said, reaching out with his good arm to pull Bob's boxers down.

Bob rose to his knees and wiggled until his boxers slid over his hips. His large cock stood at attention. He wanted to say something when Steve slid even nearer.

"Keep that way." And Steve closed his mouth over Bob's cock, licking and kissing his way along the shaft.

"My God, what are you doing to me?" Bob moaned. He was on fire. Steve's soft lips gave him a sensation he had never felt before. The women he had made love with in the past were totally forgotten. This was the way it should have been all along! He stroked Steve's dark hair, watching his head move up and down.

Suddenly he pulled back. "Wait a sec."

Steve made a sucking sound when his mouth came off Bob's cock. Steve's lips were wet with saliva. "Don't you like what I'm doing?"

"On the contrary. But what about a different position?" Bob raised his eyebrows suggestively, and Steve nodded. Lying in sixty-nine position gave them the best access to show their love to each other for the first time.

Braced on an elbow, Bob took Steve in hand, feeling the soft flesh that hardened further under his touch. With gentle strokes, he teased and caressed Steve's cock.

Steve moaned. "Bob, if you keep doing that, I'm going to come right away. Come here." Steve nudged him to travel south again. "Need you there, pal," he said, licking Bob's shaft in one long move.

Bob released Steve's cock and paid attention to his scrotum, playing with the wiry dark hair. He couldn't resist burying his nose in Steve's crotch. This was his lover, his scent, the smell of sex.

Getting more aroused by Steve's ministrations, Bob kissed his way up to the navel. "Hello, again," he whispered.

Smiling, Bob marveled at the sensation of giving and receiving so much pleasure. Steve did wonderful things with Bob's throbbing cock, engulfing him with his mouth.

Bob wished this moment would last forever. He cupped Steve's hard cock, and the furry balls seemed to tighten with every stroke Bob made. Steve moaned with pleasure, proving that Bob was doing all the right things for his lover. When the cock in Bob's hands swelled even more, he took it into his mouth and sucked vigorously.

Bob felt Steve tense, and then a gush of warm fluid filled his mouth. He was overwhelmed and worried that he would choke. Releasing Steve from his mouth, Bob used his hand to milk him until the last drop left the softening cock. Bob gasped when Steve blew air over the crown of his erection, and he went off like a rocket. Exhausted, he lay on Steve's thighs, catching his breath. Both he and Steve were slicked with sweat.

"Thanks." Steve looked down at him, love shining from his eyes.

"Thank *you!*" Bob crawled over to curl into Steve's good arm. He thought of cleaning up the mess they'd made in the bed, but that could wait. Bob pulled the cover over their heated bodies, then he embraced Steve. "Everything okay with your arm?"

Steve answered sleepily, "I've never felt better in my life."

"Tell me about it." Bob sealed Steve's mouth with a deep kiss.

LATER THAT morning Rollins closed the last of the reports from the drug-related deaths and put them aside. "That's it!" He looked at Steve and Bob, sitting in front of his desk. "You two have been really busy. I am proud that you were able to track down the men who brought Blue Rocket to the streets and caused the deaths of nine people."

"What probably killed them was that the drug was too strong and pure," Bob said and took a sip from his hot coffee.

Rollins nodded. "It killed nine young people who had preexisting health problems, like a heart condition."

"What we need to know is"—Steve squirmed in his chair, touching his sore arm—"what happened to Freddie and Chris? When we arrested Sanders yesterday, he said they were going to check on the dead bodies. Did anyone pick them up?" He looked at Bob. "Chris must have figured out by now that Glassman was arrested."

"Freddie is in danger," Bob said. He didn't want to imagine what had happened to Freddie. Freddie had saved their lives, and now he needed their help.

"Freddie Garner is a clever guy." Rollins smiled fondly. "When he and Chris were on their way to North Park, he pretended something was wrong with the car. They stopped at the next gas station."

Steve listened in openmouthed fascination. "What happened?"

Bob bent forward. "Cap, don't keep us in suspense. Is Freddie safe?"

Rollins cleared his throat. "Yes. He slipped away from Barber after he'd pretended to go to the restroom. He was able to call the police. Both men were busted and are awaiting their interrogation."

"But Freddie didn't do anything!" Steve said.

Rollins waved his hand to shut them up. "Of course not. We want to protect Freddie's undercover identity. So he's being treated like a criminal right now."

"There's still a hell of a lot of Blue Rocket out there. We're afraid that some users have been selling it for an inflated price on the street." Bob took a deep breath. "We could have more deaths or psychotic breaks from users. Once the addicts get their hands on it, there's no stopping people from making more, now that Glassman is out of business."

"We need to get the names of the people Glassman distributed the drug to." Steve started pacing around.

"The bank statements that were found in the raid on the club prove that Sanders was financing Glassman's drug business, and Barber was helping bring in models and actors by luring them with Blue Rocket," Bob added.

"And they killed Randolph, who decided to bust up the drug organization." Steve stopped in front of Rollins's desk, fumbling with his sling.

"How's your arm, Steve? Still hurting?" Rollins asked with a frown.

"Much better, sir, I don't feel any pain, just a bit uncomfortable with the sling and all."

Rollins nodded and looked from Steve to Bob. "Anything wrong between you two?"

Bob blushed. "Everything's okay. The whole thing took a toll on us, and we're still tired...."

"You'll get some days off," Rollins said, fiddling with his tie. "Steve's on sick leave anyway."

Bob glanced at Steve with a slight grin. When he was in public, he still felt a weird embarrassment thinking about what had changed the night before. Could Rollins possibly read it in their body language? He and Steve usually sat practically in the same chair, but today they were about as far apart as they could be in Rollins's small office.

Steve smiled at Rollins. "Thanks for the days off. But first I'd like to have a word with Sanders. We have the weapon used on Randolph Foreman. Did Sanders admit that he killed Randolph?"

Rollins shook his head. "Steve, I don't want you to be the one who interrogates Sanders. He stabbed you. You are a victim."

"I'm fully capable of handling things," Steve objected.

"I'm sure Sanders will claim he has an alibi for last Wednesday. He's probably still saying he was with a girl until they arrived at Glassman's practice." Bob got up and walked around the table to take a look at the case folder.

Rollins leafed through the pages. "Myers did the first questioning yesterday. Sanders repeated that he was with...." Rollins searched for the statement Sanders made.

"Gloria Thumbnail. Here, Captain." Bob pointed to a name at the end of the report. "We already interviewed her once, and she corroborated his alibi."

"That won't help him a lot." Rollins pointed at another page. "Ballistics found out that the weapon Sanders used on you is the same gun Randolph Foreman was killed with. The bullet removed from Foreman's head was from Sanders's Colt."

"I'm sure that Sanders killed Randolph!" Steve said, sounding determined. "Randolph knew all about Blue Rocket and who was distributing it. When he lost his lover Evan, he was certain that Sanders was responsible and must have decided to tell the police."

"That was the reason Randolph offered to be a snitch. I wonder what Chris Barber had to do with the whole affair?" Bob pinched his nose tiredly. Tying up the loose ends was always complicated.

"We'll find out," Rollins said grimly.

"It sure looked like Enrico could have done it out of spite at first," Steve said, taking the cup from Bob and looking disappointed when he saw it was empty.

Rollins scribbled on a sheet of paper. "I'll have an officer bring Gloria Thumbnail in for further questioning and charge her with perjury if she refuses to tell the truth. We have to get the goods on Sanders to charge him with first-degree murder."

"Keep us in the loop, sir." Bob threw the empty coffee cup in the trash, opened the office door, and let Steve go out first.

Rollins smiled. Smiling back as he closed the door, Bob wondered what Rollins would think if he knew about what he and Steve had done last night.

"NOW WE got him!" Steve bounced out of the interrogation room where Gloria Thumbnail had just been questioned.

"You did a very good bad cop." Bob followed him, not trying to hide his admiration for Steve's butt in those tight jeans.

"Yeah, she had to confess that she only joined Sanders in Santa Barbara, and not a minute earlier." Steve grinned.

"All I had to do was tell her Sanders used the weapon in a crime and ask her if she wanted to be treated as an accomplice. Then she told the truth." Bob shrugged and put his hand on Steve's back. "Can't wait to see Sanders in court."

"And Chris as well. I bet he helped Sanders do the dirty work." Steve hurried. "I'm hungry. The special burger at Larry's is on me. And for dessert…."

The look he sent Bob gave Bob wobbly legs.

Chapter Fifteen

IT WAS five months later, on a rainy February morning, and Bob stopped his old Mercedes at the repair shop. "Hey, Sam, something's wrong with the brakes. Can you check them, please? I have time, I can wait."

Sam the mechanic shuffled around the car, bending down to check the brakes. "Forget it, Curry. This car needs more attention than just fixing the brakes." He shook his head.

"Damn!" Bob looked at his watch. "I'll be late for the briefing with Rollins."

"Sorry, man." Sam shrugged, wiping his oily hands on his overalls.

LOOKING FOR a cab, Bob walked along the street, pulling his collar up against the rain. In spite of it, he felt happy and relieved. Just the day before, Sanders and Chris Barber had been sentenced for murder and attempted murder respectively.

As it turned out, the meeting Randolph went to after leaving Steve and Enrico had evolved into a shouting match with his colleagues. He told Sanders and Barber that he intended to go to the police with the information that they were manufacturing Blue Rocket. So after he left, they followed him home, caught him in a dark corner of the park, and Sanders shot him. Chris Barber had helped hide the corpse.

Ruben Glassman had admitted that he had experimented with different combinations of amphetamines to create Blue Rocket. He was in jail, and luckily no other chemist had figured out the components accurately enough to continue making the drug. Blue Rocket had vanished from the streets.

Bob took a deep breath. The peace wouldn't last long before the next drug would hit the market.

He saw a couple of men hanging a huge poster on the side of a construction site fence across from Sam's garage. Bob felt sorry they had to work in the rain… until he looked at the poster. The sight took his breath away.

It was a picture of Steve, larger than life, posing in tight-fitting trunks!

Large blue letters scrawled across the top of the poster read "For men—the new trend in beach fashion!"

Bob rubbed his eyes to make sure he wasn't dreaming. "Oh, man. Steve, if you saw this," Bob moaned, rooted to the spot.

One of the workers headed back to their van. He looked at Bob and smiled. "If I were a girl, I wouldn't hesitate a minute. A great model, isn't he?"

Bob couldn't help smiling mischievously. "Absolutely."

He laughed, half turned on and half mortified.

Thirty minutes later, Bob walked into the precinct. He went straight to the squad room, where he could hear excited voices.

"Bob! You have to see this!" Police secretary Millie Swanson left the crowd of officers, waving the magazine in her hand. "It's Steve! He's posing in the new swimsuits! Look, I couldn't believe my eyes. He's so sexy!" Out of breath, she beamed at Bob.

Bob grabbed the magazine out of her hand, almost too roughly. "If Steve sees that, he'll have a heart attack!" Bob said, turning the pages. Memories of the day of the photo shoot came back in a rush. The photos were fantastic. Steve's sensual eroticism radiated off the glossy page. Bob thought Steve was the most gorgeous man in the world, but he couldn't say so aloud. He was about to put the magazine into his desk when the doors swung open, and Steve came in.

Every cop in the room turned toward him. Steve stopped. "What's going on here? I feel like a felon on the way to have a mug shot."

"You mean a photo shoot," Millie burst out. "Bob, show him the pictures!"

Bob thought about gagging her for bringing it up. He glanced at Myers, Robinson, and the other officers in the room. They were suddenly silent. They all looked from Steve to Bob and back again.

"What's going on here?" Steve asked again.

"I have something to tell you privately." Bob put his arm around Steve's shoulder to pull him out of the room.

"Don't forget the magazine!" Millie called. She grabbed *Modern Man* off Bob's desk and handed it to him. She beamed at Steve, nudging him in the side. "Steve, you are the most beautiful cop in beachwear, believe me!"

"What?" Steve tried to resist, but Bob forced him out of the room. "Bob, tell me, what's this all about?" Steve stopped, looking horrified. It was as if a light bulb went on in his head. "Oh no," he groaned, following Bob into the men's room.

Bob locked the door behind them and held up the magazine. The cover shot was Steve in Bermudas, playing with a ball. There were seven pages in the layout, all in bright, sunny color. Steve pretending to run along the beach, the tight trunks revealing his muscular body, Steve laughing in a barely there suit, Steve jumping up as if to spike a volleyball, the red trunks accenting his flat belly.

"I've never seen a better-looking model," Bob said honestly.

Steve was obviously not in the mood to listen to sweet words. "Do you know how I felt posing in that studio, with nothing on except those trunks? My body was oiled and my hair was clotted with gel." Steve shuddered.

Despite the public place, Bob pulled his partner close.

Steve resisted at first, but with a long sigh, he surrendered and let his head fall against Bob's chest. After a moment he lifted his head. "I don't know how Randolph could have sent the pictures to the magazine so quickly. He was killed that night," he mumbled.

"He did it. Now you have to deal with the pictures," Bob said with a touch of humor. "But honestly, you should be proud. You look great, and Randolph's latest model is a real keeper." Bob cupped Steve's cheek and dropped a kiss on his forehead.

"Hey, is that all?" Steve complained playfully.

Bob grinned and kissed his lover on the lips. The sensation made his legs wobbly, and he could have stayed that way forever.

Persistent knocking on the door interrupted their meeting.

"See you!" Steve whispered. He handed Bob the key for the Thunderbird and ducked into a stall.

"Don't let me wait too long." Bob smiled and unlocked the door, shoving the magazine in his jacket pocket.

Bob went down to the garage and waited in the car, flipping through the magazine layout again. He wanted to keep these pictures forever. Grinning, he got an idea. He had a nice gift for Steve in mind for Valentine's Day.

"YOU'RE LATE. Did you get your car back? What did Sam charge for trying to repair the old model?" Steve asked, sprawled on his couch, watching TV.

"It's like new." Bob dropped the keys on the little shelf next to the front door and carried the brown bag under his arm to the kitchen.

"You got something for dinner? I'm starving," Steve said.

Bob heard him get up and come to the kitchen. "Surprise, surprise!" Bob said, taking two boxes out of the bag.

"Mmm, it smells good. What is it?" Steve sniffed with appreciation and licked his lips.

Bob turned his head and met Steve's mouth for a lingering kiss.

"It's hot 'n' spicy," Bob said into Steve's mouth.

Steve laughed. "Sure, that's what I am."

"Dummy. It's from the new Mexican restaurant. Burritos and enchiladas, with extra sauce. Help yourself. It's still warm." Bob handed Steve the boxes, along with a knife and fork.

"What else is there in your bag?" Always curious, Steve took a peek.

"That's for dessert." Gently Bob shoved Steve out of the kitchen. "Wait! I forgot the wine. Callaway red, a cabernet sauvignon." He poured the dark red wine into two elegant glasses.

"That sounds inviting." Steve swaggered to the dining table, put the food out, and sat down.

"To life and love!" Bob toasted. Steve smiled broadly. They clinked glasses and enjoyed their meal.

"YOU'RE SPOILING me," Steve said, content, leaning back against the couch cushions.

"Happy Valentine's Day, Steve," Bob said, sitting very close to him. It was hard not to smile from ear to ear, thinking about the dessert he had for Steve.

"Oh yes, don't you think that I forgot." Steve sprawled across Bob's lap. "I got something for you. Let me get it." He draped himself completely over Bob, reaching down under the couch.

Bob couldn't resist. He lifted Steve's shirt to tease a ticklish spot.

"Ahhh, you're mean." Steve wriggled on Bob's lap.

Bob couldn't get enough of the strong body pressing against him.

"Got it!" Steve squirmed away from his tormenter and presented Bob with the package he'd retrieved from under the couch. "For you," he said, still lounging on Bob's lap.

"Hope I deserve it." Bob smiled, not too interested in the gift. Steve looked so gorgeous in his lap, with his tight jeans appearing painted on his body. "You're distracting me here," Bob whispered, running his hand down Steve's shirt and unbuttoning it.

Steve sat up. He snaked his arm around Bob's neck. Bob purred when Steve kissed his face, wandering over to his earlobe. Steve pressed his tongue into Bob's ear, tickling him there.

Bob giggled and forced himself to pull back. "Wait a sec, we can't miss the dessert. It's my Valentine's gift for you."

Steve looked at him with lust. "I'm not hungry for anything but you," he moaned, embracing Bob.

More determined this time, Bob shoved him aside, ignoring Steve's complaint. "I've got something for you too. We can open our Valentine's gifts at the same time. That should be fun." Bob hurried back into the kitchen and returned with a little package.

"That doesn't look like a dessert," Steve said, weighing the lightweight box in his hand. He looked at Bob. "Open your gift first. It's only a little something, but I want to see your face."

Bob opened the box wrapped in white paper printed with pink hearts and held up a small electronic device. "What is it?" he asked, puzzled.

"Dummy. It's a new horn for your precious car. It plays the 'Colonel Bogey March.'" Steve hummed the familiar tune.

"Really funny. Thanks." Bob pointed to his package for Steve. "Now you."

"Let me guess—a new Yamamoto watch." Steve shook the package carefully.

"I'm sorry, no." Bob hoped Steve wouldn't be offended or irritated. It had seemed like a great idea yesterday.

Steve ripped off the wrapping paper. He opened the small box and didn't say anything, just stared at the contents.

"Do you like it?" Bob heard his own voice. He didn't sound confident at all.

"There's nothing to this. It wouldn't cover anything." Steve held up a black thong with two fingers, as if it could explode at any second.

Bob cleared his throat. "When I saw you posing in that magazine, I wished you could do that for me, as my personal model." He touched the silky fabric. "So I bought this for you."

"You must be nuts, Bob! I'm no model, and I'm never posing like that again," Steve said with determination. He dropped the thong into the box and shifted to the edge of the couch to get some distance between them.

Crushed, Bob sighed. "I'm sorry. Yesterday it seemed like a great idea." No sexy lingerie for Steve, then. "Give me the thong. I'll return it tomorrow." Bob grabbed the box, but Steve plucked the thong out, holding it tightly.

"What now?" Bob asked, puzzled.

Steve had a sudden, mischievous smile. He turned the black underwear back and forth as if pondering how well it would fit him. "Well, I'm thinking about doing my lover a favor. If you do something for me in return." He dangled the thong in front of Bob's face.

Bob clasped Steve's hand to stop him. "What is it?" He knew he sounded suspicious, although he would do anything for Steve.

"Promise me you'll look for another car. That old Mercedes has let you down so many times. We'll find something suitable for you, and the new horn will be the icing on the cake." Steve took the horn out of the package and pressed the button.

The first eight notes of the whistling theme from *The Bridge on the River Kwai* rang out. Bob reared back in astonishment. There was no way he was having that horn on his car!

"It's great, isn't it?" Steve beamed. "It's unforgettable." He pushed the button again. "You can make it even louder. You wanna hear?"

"No, thanks." Bob took a deep breath. "I promise to look for another car, though. Maybe a BMW."

"Whatever you wish." Steve moved closer, pushing Bob back until Steve lay on top of him. "So you want me to be your model?" Steve swung the thong around his forefinger.

Bob embraced Steve, feeling every muscle against him. He moaned. "Love, get rid of your jeans, I'm ready for the show."

Steve sat down directly on top of the bulge in Bob's groin. He chuckled. "Hey, I love this."

Bob caught Steve's mouth in a fierce kiss. He didn't want to let go, but when Steve scrambled off the couch, Bob didn't hold him back. He was looking forward to his personal fashion show, performed by his partner and lover.

Steve disappeared into the bathroom, swinging the thong over his head.

Bob grinned, admiring Steve's grace. Steve moved like a dancer even when he was walking. And when he was on the dance floor, he outperformed every other dancer there. Bob loved to watch his friend dance and had always wished he could have a private show.

Some music! Bob needed a song Steve liked for the performance. Rummaging in Steve's CD rack, Bob found some of Steve's favorites. But none of them was exactly right for thong modeling.

"That's it!" Bob held up Tom Jones's "You Can Leave Your Hat On." Full of anticipation, he put the CD in the player. The sound filled the room, and Bob leaned back, his jeans becoming tight across the groin area. He reached down, trying to adjust himself more comfortably.

Slowly the bathroom door opened, and Steve came out.

Bob was disappointed. Steve was still wearing his jeans and unbuttoned shirt.

"I thought…," Bob started but closed his mouth when he saw Steve swaggering across the room, swaying smoothly to the music.

Steve glanced at Bob from under his long dark lashes, playing with his belt buckle. Bob caught his breath. Steve looked so sexy and strong. Bob couldn't keep his eyes off the man dancing in front of him.

"Wait a sec." Steve stopped dancing and walked over to the window to draw the blinds.

"Never mind," Bob whispered. He was astonished that Steve was going to do a striptease for him!

Normally Steve wasn't shy at all, but this was no ordinary day. This was a celebration of their new relationship. To encourage Steve he clapped his hands and sang along with the song, telling Steve to keep his hat on.

"You bet!" Steve said with a sassy wiggle. His blue eyes sparkled when he unbuckled the buckle and then the top button of his jeans.

Bob waited for them to come down, but instead Steve lifted his shirt, tearing one button off completely. It flew across the room and landed on the coffee table. The shirt followed, covering Bob's head.

Bob mumbled good-naturedly from under the shirt. Inhaling Steve's scent, Bob savored the short moment before he threw the shirt aside to get a better look at the show.

Steve moved his hips sensually, his hands roaming freely over his chest. His fingers lingered on his nipples, teasing them.

Very aroused, Bob searched Steve's eyes, seeing excitement and love there. *How do I deserve you? What you do to me is just incredible. I'm the luckiest guy on earth.*

The song was about moving your limbs and going with the music. Life is only worth it when you love somebody.

Steve glided across the room with some quick little dance steps. He flung off one shoe and bent down to get rid of his blue sock. He threw it up in the air. The sock landed on the lamp, making the room go slightly darker.

"Nice move." Bob smiled, ready to catch the other sock.

Steve shimmied away. The second shoe was swiftly toed off and kicked under the table, sock and all. In his bare feet, Steve danced to the music, waving his arms, just as Tom Jones had sung.

Bob loved seeing the fine sheen of sweat on Steve's chest hair. "Come on, show me what I'm waiting for," Bob cheered, encouraging him.

Slowly Steve pushed his jeans over his hips. He struggled with the tight denim and almost lost his balance. Bob was ready to catch him, but Steve regained his stance. The jeans came down, and Steve carefully stepped out of them. He stood directly in front of Bob with his legs spread, the black thong hardly covering the promising bulge.

"Wow." Bob whistled, impressed. He absorbed Steve's exotic beauty with appreciation.

Bob was tempted to reach out to Steve, to feel the sweaty skin beneath his hands and stroke the fine hairline that led from the navel downward. He bent forward to catch him, but Steve turned around and danced away from him, wiggling his nearly naked ass.

"Hey, where are you going?" Bob called, more than a little turned on.

Steve grabbed something from the closet, his lean body shining from the light in the hall.

"What the hell?" Bob stood up to get a better view.

Steve came back with his head bowed so that his face was not visible under the cowboy hat.

"What does it say about that hat in the song?" Steve tipped the hat brim with one finger, moving his hips invitingly.

"You can leave your hat on—and only that!" Bob said, unable to wait any longer. "Come here," he said huskily, putting his hands on Steve's hips. The warmth of Steve's flesh seeped into Bob. He found the thin cord that held the thong in place and pulled it down.

"Bob…," Steve said almost shyly, looking down at his groin.

Bob dropped to his knees. Ignoring the erect cock, he looked up, running his hand up to Steve's navel, caressing the delicate line of hair.

Steve shivered.

"Are you cold?" Bob asked, keeping his hand on Steve's abdomen.

"Not exactly." Steve ran his fingers through Bob's hair, encouraging him to do more exploration.

Bob kissed his way up the inner thighs, tasting the sweaty skin before he stopped at Steve's groin. Steve groaned, and Bob pulled him closer, resting his hands on Steve's hips. Getting closer to the object of his desire, he nuzzled his nose in the wiry hair at the base of Steve's cock.

"Bob, you're killing me here!" Gentle hands urged Bob to go a bit further.

"Glad to oblige," Bob mumbled. He bent his head and found the hot balls, tense and at the same time, so tender and vulnerable. He used his tongue to lick and taste and then lightly scrape with his teeth.

"No," Steve whimpered.

Bob immediately stopped. "Did I hurt you?" he whispered against Steve's skin. He hadn't intended to do any harm to Steve.

"Don't you dare!" Forcefully, Steve grabbed Bob's head to put it back in the previous position. "That was so—so amazing! Keep going!"

Bob felt light-headed all of a sudden. He had done the right thing, which was all that mattered. Encouraged to finish what he had started, Bob took one ball in his mouth, fondling it with tongue and lips. He heard Steve moan, and joy filled him that he could pleasure his partner this way.

"If you keep going, I can't hold on much longer," Steve gasped.

Knowing Steve was on the edge, Bob slowed down. "We have all the time in the world, don't we?"

"Unless you let me wait too long." Hungrily, Steve moved his hips forward, and his fully aroused cock grazed Bob's face.

Bob caught the sturdy shaft, enclosing it with his mouth. Steve hissed with need. Bob ran his tongue up and down the length, the hardened yet silky flesh filling his mouth. Unconditionally happy, he sucked Steve's shaft. He'd never believed that he would enjoy giving head to a man, but it was one of the most glorious moments of his life.

Steve cradled Bob's head, tightening his grip when Bob's tongue teased his leaking slit.

"Bob…." The name was barely audible, but Bob knew how close Steve was.

Bob tasted the bitter precome and decided to swallow Steve entirely. Before they'd started, he'd been worried that he might choke on Steve's impressive length, but since that hadn't happened, he was eager to try more daring techniques.

As he enveloped his lover's arousal, Bob used his teeth to gently increase the pressure on Steve. He heard moans and a whimper and knew Steve was about to climax.

In one smooth movement, Bob relaxed his throat and took the full length. Steve seemed to hesitate for a second. Bob didn't let up. He licked and bit at the firm flesh in his mouth. When he felt Steve stiffen under his hands, Bob grabbed Steve's ass with both hands, squeezing tightly.

Hot fluid filled his throat. Bob swallowed and tried not to choke. Steve's cock softened as it released the load. Tenderly, Bob let his lips wander along the length before he released him.

"You still alive?" Steve croaked, stroking Bob's sweaty face.

"Yeah, how about you?" Bob looked up at him.

"I have no words. Bob, you're incredible." Steve crouched in front of Bob, reaching out to help him up.

Bob tried, but his knees had cramped as if objecting to the uncomfortable position. He groaned and dropped down on his butt, stretching out his legs.

"Not the most comfortable position in the world," Steve said with a smirk.

"Nothing to worry about," Bob said. The sight of Steve, naked, made him very aware of his own arousal. He shifted to adjust his pants.

"Come on." Steve's strong arms enveloped him, and Bob carefully stood.

Sneaking a kiss from Steve, Bob grinned. "Let's get more comfortable, huh?" He put his arm around Steve's waist and pointed to the bedroom.

Playfully Steve bumped him, his flaccid cock dangling in Bob's direction. "Let me show you now how much I love you." He grabbed Bob's belt buckle and unbuckled it dexterously.

"You already showed me your love today." Bob tapped Steve's hat, which sat at a rakish angle on his head.

"You mean...?" Steve paused in the middle of opening Bob's zipper.

"Yeah, posing in that tiny piece of cloth meant a lot to me." Bob looked fondly at Steve.

"Oh, you're welcome. And now...." Steve pushed him gently into the bedroom and up against the edge of the bed. Pulling the jeans down over Bob's slim hips, he grinned hugely at the bulge in Bob's boxers. "You're at my mercy now, Bob. I want you to be *my* model." Steve nudged Bob onto his back on the bed.

"A model? Don't you dare!" Bob protested.

Ignoring him, Steve tugged the boxers down. Bob's cock greeted him in all its gorgeousness.

Bob's arousal nearly peaked at the sight of Steve dominating him. He took a deep breath, excited at the prospect of Steve going down on him as he had just done to Steve.

"And you can leave your hat on," Steve hummed, placing his hat over Bob's cock.

"What?" Bob started when Steve sealed his mouth with a passionate kiss.

STAR NOBLE started writing short stories as a teenager and hasn't stopped since. When she found the Internet and the world of gay romance she was hooked.

She has been participating in an online writing community for seven years and is looking forward to having her work published.

When she isn't writing romantic stories about beautiful men, she's teaching in Germany. Her other hobbies are reading, singing, travelling, drawing, and dancing.

You can contact her at moonlight17@t-online.de.

http://www.dreamspinnerpress.com

SCOTTY CADE

THE ROYAL STREET HEIST

http://www.dreamspinnerpress.com

A JEFF WOODS MYSTERY

ATTACHMEN
STRINGS

CHRIS T. KAT

http://www.dreamspinnerpress.com

Broken
MERCIES

Lucy Marker

http://www.dreamspinnerpress.com

UNDERCOVER
Addiction

Hayley B. James

http://www.dreamspinnerpress.com

LOVING
Hector
John Inman